The Alewives

A plague-era tale of murder, friendship, and fine ale

Elizabeth R. Andersen

Haeddre Press

Contents

For Katers

When we were five years old, I accidentally lit you on fire at a 4th of July picnic.

Thirty-five years later, I am still grateful for your friendship, and baffled that you've stayed with me.

Hochsommer

In which a hoe has gone missing

IT WAS ONLY THE second day of the holy feast of Saint John the Baptist, and Frau Gritta, the wife of Jorges Leporteur, was sure that her children would not survive until Michaelmas. She had twelve of them, you see. Frau Berthe, the pious, primping hussy two doors down, only had four (those that lived), and they were the pride of Colmar – sweet, hardworking, intelligent, and beautiful, each one of them. Gritta's lank-haired children were all destined to be grifters, from Lisette, the eldest, to what's-her-name, the youngest, who Gritta only recently managed to detach from the teat.

It didn't matter. None of her children would survive anyhow. If Gritta didn't thrash them into oblivion, then starvation would get them first. She pondered this as she scattered a pile of weeds and barley hulls for the hens that scratched alongside her large but shabby house on Trench Lane in Les Tanneurs.

Colmar, known for its fine wines and rich, abundant soil, was a pretty city full of fine people...except those who lived in Les Tanneurs – the tanners' quarter. Les Tanneurs contained the city's dyers, tanners, and leatherworks, conveniently located downstream and downwind of the wealthy burghers' homes near the church and the priory of the Dominicans, and the poorest occupants of Les Tanneurs lived on Trench Lane, which took its name from the deep-walled ditch that furrowed the center of the street. In dry times, the ditch filled with dung and other refuse that tripped passersby, but when the rains fell, it became a temporary stream that shunted filthy water into the canals.

Those that didn't live in Les Tanneurs called it "the stinkards."

People told Gritta she was fortunate. No one in her family, including herself and good-for-nothing Jorges, had died of the Great Pestilence, the plague of buboes that had ravaged the whole of the Rhineland, from Annecy to Frankfurt. Some even claimed that the pestilence stretched throughout the whole of the earth, like a demon from hell, holding all of God's creatures in its grip of death and horror. The intact survival of such a large family was an immense rarity, even in her city, which had not had the worst of it. Not like Strassburg.

Her children – those that were old enough – worked odd jobs around the city, running errands, mucking out stalls in the innkeeper's stables, or swindling kind-hearted traders on market days. Her eldest daughter, Lisette, worked as a washerwoman at Lord Frider's castle in the hills, keeping the old nobleman distracted while he waited for Lady Marguerite to give birth. Gritta always knew Lisette's pretty face would serve her well someday, and she didn't begrudge the girl this little indiscretion. It would never come back to benefit them, but it couldn't hurt them either. After all, how far could they sink below their present station? Jorges worked as a porter at the docks in Vogelgrun when there was a need, and after the pestilence, there was far less need. Sometimes he helped move barrows of foul, stinking animal soil used by the tanners, or worked in Lord Frider's fields, but most of the time he spent his days curled up in a pile of straw near the fire, snoring in a cloud of wine fumes.

One of her children strolled lazily into the dooryard, kicking up little puffs of dust at each step. But which one was it? Gritta mentally listed her children's names, trying to assign the correct one to the long-faced lad. Urbe, Anstett, Mattheus, Egilhard…ah, of course, it was Lonel.

Tall and lean as a barley straw, with a perpetually bemused expression on his face, Lonel was the pebble in Gritta's shoe and the fly in her porridge. Always in trouble, just like his father, but with the quickest laugh and the easiest smile, Lonel always seemed to be telling a joke or laughing at one. But while he charmed and flirted with his golden tongue, he was usually stealing food or money with his roving hands.

Gritta planted hands on hips that were once round and soft, now bony and sharp from years of sorrow and starvation, and narrowed her eyes in her sternest fashion.

"Well then, my best garden hoe has gone missing. I suppose you did something with it, did you?"

"Ma," Lonel laughed, "why would I take your hoe?"

"Why indeed. I shouldn't have asked, for I know you've never done a lick of work in your life."

Lonel shrugged in acknowledgment. He wore his notorious laziness like a badge of pride in Les Tanneurs. When a tanner asked for help lifting the hides from one of the soaking pits, Lonel just laughed. When a goodwife struggled beneath a load of firewood or a basket of vegetables, Lonel would slink away. The only time he ever seemed to present himself amongst his neighbors was to observe one of the many illegal games of stones and bones, or else he would show up when a tinker or a new trader came to town, brandishing coins that Gritta knew were ill-gotten.

"It's washing day and the girls are down at the riverbank, so I'm going round with Gerhard to find me a wife. Don't mind, do you?" Lonel drawled.

"What? Better you had catch eels instead of a wife, or we'll have no supper tonight."

"Thanks, Ma!" Lonel retreated before Gritta could question him further.

"No young maid would want you for a husband until you learn to show your ma some respect!" she shouted after him.

Gritta understood the futility of this complaint but felt she must voice it all the same, to assert herself as someone who had a few years of experience above this child. Lonel stopped and laughed.

"You're funny, Ma! The washing girls aren't maidens – they can't even clean their reputations."

"Hi! Your sister is one of those washing women!"

"Aye, that's how I know!" Lonel called back without looking over his shoulder. As he retreated, his slim silhouette wavered in the late afternoon heat.

If this had been her firstborn, Gritta might have slumped wearily back into the house and mourned for the reputation of her legacy. But Lonel was only her sixth-born. Most days, she didn't remember that he still lived under her roof, if he came home at all. She supposed this might make her a deficient mother, and then she figured that it didn't matter. If Lonel were to wed, she would have an excuse to toss him out, and that would be one less mouth to feed. Who cared if he took an unchaste washerwoman for a wife?

A faint whiff of a song drifted on a puff of hot wind and into Gritta's ears. She froze, the chickens at her feet scratching about restlessly, the problem of the missing hoe forgotten.

"In the boozer, you're a loser, if the dice you're shaking!"

The sultry summer heat rose in waves from the dusty dooryard, but the shadows grew long as the day pulled back to allow the night to advance. As the singing drew closer, Gritta groaned. Jorges was on his way home from the fields, his drunken voice ringing out for the whole neighborhood to hear. She quickly pulled the drying swaddling rags from the tree branches where she hung them in the sun to bleach and hurried into the house, slamming the door. Jorges' singing grew louder and more boisterous.

"You'll get hurt and lose your shirt and sit there cold an' quaking!"

When he burst through the door, Gritta had sliced a loaf of brown rye bread and spread it with a thick smear of soft cheese from their little goat. Jorges dropped heavily into a chair at the head of the table. He had the top of his tunic untied, showing a skinny chest of leathery skin, and bits of straw dangled from his untidy brown hair. He flashed a crooked smile at his wife.

"Gritta, my dove, the fields were harsh today. So much heat. It is too much for a man to bear."

Gritta pressed her lips and held out her hand. "Give it here, then."

"Give what where?"

"Your wages. Were you paid in coppers or something else today?"

"Ah, yes." Jorges reached into the shabby leather sack that still hung at his waist and pulled out a handful of wilted poppies, presenting them to her with a flourish.

"Flowers o' the field, but they are not as beautiful as you, my dove." Then he waited, a grin splitting his craggy face.

"Where's the money, Jorges?" Gritta circled him. "Did you receive grain? Goods? You were gone all day, and now I want to see what you received for it."

"I was paid with a jar of the finest wine that Lord Frider's cellarer had to offer." He smacked his lips.

"Oh? And where is this fine wine now?"

"Had to quench my thirst. It was hot as a forge in the fields, as I said. Lord Frider has the largest crop o' barley in the valley, and it took a fair effort for us all to harvest. Why, we were parched and crying out for rain when it was all over, and then the cellarer appeared with his nectar of heaven. I prayed to the Lord God for water, but as only wine was available, I had to drink it – for my health, you see. It was a miracle, it was."

Gritta closed her eyes, her mouth set in a firm line. She didn't know why she even asked, as the answer was clearly in front of her; the wine fumes radiated from Jorges' body, overpowering the smell of the tannery next door. He reached out a hand and grabbed the skirt of her threadbare cotte, pulling her to his lap.

"Here now, old girl, don't fret yourself. I reckon I can make you feel better if you give me a chance." He waggled an unkempt eyebrow at her.

"Of course," Gritta smiled, "let me pour you a drink first."

She rummaged in the cupboard and found a jar of old wine, so thick and foul that she almost had a mind to run it through a bit of cloth to strain the clumps of debris out first. Filling Jorges' cup to the top, she presented it to him and left the jar on the table. Jorges poured himself another when he had finished, and Gritta arranged a wimple over her hair.

"I'm off visiting," she announced.

"S'that?" Jorges' eyelids were already beginning to slip downward.

"Feed the children, will you?" she called sweetly before she slipped out of the house into the twilight.

Cats, large and small

In which Colmar gains a new widow

A CROSS THE DUSTY LANE, the wavering flame of a rushlight glowed from an open doorway that belonged to Frau Appel Schneider. An old ginger cat lazed on the threshold, taking in the remnants of heat that radiated from the wattle and daub walls, which Appel's husband had painted bright yellow. That was years ago, of course, and the paint now flaked off, leaving exposed brown patches of plaster and woven willow twigs. After the hand of the Great Pestilence took him, Appel buried her husband in the garden behind the house because there was no more space in the consecrated ground of the cemetery where the bodies were stacked like logs under the sod. A local priest had been kind enough to bless the dirt in her garden, so she had enough room to lay her only daughter's bones to rest a few weeks later, along with her infant grandson and the little orphan boy who served as their hired hand. Of her family, Appel was the only one who survived. Her story was neither unusual nor pitysome after the Great Pestilence. Times were hard for everyone.

Gritta peeked through the open door. She no longer worried about Appel as she did a year ago when things were so terrible for all of them in Colmar, but for a moment, the profound silence in the house frightened her. Not long ago, when a house fell silent, you knew what had happened before you even looked in the window. How many times in the preceding years had she stopped in to check on a neighbor only to find them dead, their flesh pocked with sores? How many times had the wail of a new orphan been met with exhausted indifference from his neighbors? Not enough times for her to grow accustomed to the sound. She crossed herself for protection from the Devil and stepped inside.

"Appel dear, are you in?"

Silence. The cat stood, stretched, and began to wind himself between her ankles. Gritta looked around the room. It was simple, like all houses in Colmar that didn't belong to the wealthy burghers or the highborn – walls of yellowing plaster; a dark, heavy-beamed ceiling; and a generous hearth of soot-blackened stones from the Rhine. Appel's husband had been a well-respected tanner before the pestilence took him, and so they could afford more finery than most; a bench of carved and painted oak stood near the fire, a few tapestries hung on the walls – finely stitched with Appel's own embroidery – and there was a chipped basin of almost pure white pottery. This house even had a second floor just for sleeping.

Something thumped overhead, and Gritta jumped.

"Appel?"

She ran from the house and around the corner, where a staircase wound crookedly up the wall to the second floor. She was on the first step when Appel's smiling face appeared in the shadowed doorway above her.

"Ah, Gritta! It is a pleasure to see you, my dear." Appel pulled her apron strings around her waist and tied them snugly. They were long enough to circle her twice. As long as Gritta had known her, Appel had always been plump and jolly, but, like everyone in Colmar and the surrounding bergs, she grew scrawny and faded after the Great Pestilence. Not enough food. Not enough will to live. Her clothes hung from her body like dead leaves, but nothing could darken the brightness of her smile, despite the fact that she was getting on in her years.

Gritta grinned to hide her relief. "Sometimes I still forget that we live in better times now. I have come for your council, old friend."

"Oh? And how can I help?" Appel walked down the stairs, adjusting her skirts and running her hands over her long braid to smooth the stray silver hairs. She took Gritta's arm in hers and led her inside the house.

"My womb collects children like honey attracts ants. I seek a potion to relieve me of this uncontrolled fertility!"

Appel's face was stony for a moment. "I am a good woman of the church, Gritta. I do not deal in such sin."

Overhead, another thump startled them. Gritta quirked an eyebrow at her friend, and Appel shrugged.

"Cat."

Gritta turned and looked at the doorway, where Appel's ginger cat had resumed its languid posture.

"Well, I have more than one cat!" Appel said with irritation. Overhead, more thumps, this time in the distinct pattern of heavy footsteps. "A very large cat," she muttered.

"Would you like me to step out so you can bid farewell to your visitor?"

"No, thank you. He will see himself out through the window."

"Well then." Gritta leaned forward. "About that potion."

The shadows of the late afternoon melted into the thick, soft twilight of a sultry summer evening. Gritta and Appel shared a pitcher of wine and cackled at each other's jokes in front of the hearth. The rushlight had long since burned through, and because of the expense, there was no chance of another one, so they sweated in the flickering light of the small fire as the heat of the day's sun cocooned the house.

Gritta didn't usually take so much wine, but on this night, she enjoyed the weightless feeling of being slightly drunk. If Jorges could intoxicate himself every day, then she could do the same every fortnight. She smiled crookedly at Appel, a sudden feeling of sisterhood swelling in her heart.

"My dear neighbor, how long have we known each other?"

"As long as I have lived here, and I married my husband and moved into this house when I was still a comely young lass—" Appel hiccoughed into her hand "—and you but a babe still. I used to mind the house for your ma when she would go a'marketing, and more than one time I did redden your buttocks when you tormented your little brother."

"Aye." Gritta nodded. "He was a fine young thing, my brother, though I teased him so. It was a pity what happened to him when he fell into that well."

Appel crossed herself, and for a moment they drank in silence, the light of the fire flickering across the caverns that the Great Pestilence had carved into their faces. Gritta straightened her shoulders and squinted at her older friend.

"And all that time, you ain't never done no witchin'? Faithful as the sun rises, Appel, people do like to talk about you, and it ain't flattering."

Appel squirmed into a more comfortable position on the hard-packed earthen floor. "I ain't no witch, Gritta, and I am surprised that you asked."

"But there was that time when old Laurent the candle-dipper fell through his own thatched roof, and we thought he would never walk again. You had him on his feet in a day, but that very evening the child of Marie, the butcher's wife, died."

"Coincidence. People die, and sometimes people die on the same day that foolish old coots like Laurent the candle-dipper fall through their houses."

Gritta narrowed her eyes at her friend. "But then there was the time that you tended to Frau Widmer when she was afflicted with the Great Pestilence, and she recovered. No one recovers from the Great Pestilence, Appel. No one."

Appel took a long draw from her dish of wine. "Frau Widmer is too mean to die. The Devil doesn't want her any more than Saint Peter does."

"It was a shame, that," Gritta mused. "The neighborhood would be quieter without her."

"Don't speak such sin, Gritta."

"'Tis also a sin to rid a woman of a child, yet every woman in Colmar knows that you can do it."

"Not through potions nor incantations, my dear. I ain't no witch. I help women remain without child through revulsion."

"Tell me again, Appel, how does this 'revulsion' against children work? And what does 'revulsion' mean?"

"Ah, yes." Appel straightened and cleared her throat with the gravity of a philosopher. "You take the womb of a she-goat who has never borne a kid and carry it against you when Jorges starts a'plowing in your field. This will prevent you from getting with child again, mark me."

They looked at each other and laughed.

"Well, it works because he doesn't wish to go investigating anything so foul! You see? Revulsion!"

They roared with such laughter that they didn't hear the knock at the door. Finally, after several attempts, the door slammed open with a bang and a familiar weathered face peered in at them.

"Gritta! Where are you, woman?"

"Ah, I had better be off, then. Jorges has found me." Gritta massaged her sore shoulders and groaned as she drunkenly struggled to stand. "We were just talking about plowing, Jorges, although there will be none of that if I can't find my missing hoe."

Refreshed from his drunken nap, Jorges was uncharacteristically sure-footed. He grabbed Gritta by the arm and hefted her to her feet.

"We need your help, and here you both are, drunk as hens at a bowl of sour bread! Young Harald Kleven has gone and got himself killed, and his wife is beside herself with wailing. Can you both see to her while we take care of the body?"

Appel jumped up, immediately sober. "Harald's wife...Harald's wife..." she mused. "Is she the pretty young lass who moved here from Kleve only last year?"

"The same. The poor girl's husband was walking back to his home and was too lazy to make his way to the bridge, so he decided to vault o'er the canal with a branch."

"Well, he was a strong young lad. Surely he could have made it over the canal on a branch!" Gritta exclaimed.

"The branch broke."

"Could he not swim?" Gritta asked.

"Who knows? He was carrying a sack of hammers back to the smithy when he vaulted, so would it matter? Poor fool drowned, and once the hammers sank into the mud his body floated down to the Dominicans, but it's blocked up the stream, and now he's a'flooding all 'o the prior's fields. Oh, the prior is furious, he is! Says this will be the end 'o his cabbage crop for sure."

"Dummkopf," Gritta muttered.

"Don't go speaking 'o the prior that way, Wife. You'll bring an evil spirit on us."

"I wasn't talking about the prior. Where is the poor girl now?"

"She's at her house, and no one can console her."

Gritta and Appel exchanged a look. Now that the Great Pestilence was over, there were fewer opportunities to provide the benevolent and often unasked-for charity of the healthy. Sanctimoniousness was a rare and intoxicating liquor that must be consumed when available. The two women scrambled into action, and in no time they had their aprons straightened, their wimples fixed into place, and a basket of provisions dangling from Appel's arm. They were ready to provide comfort and cheer, whether Harald's widow wanted it or not.

Alas, poor Harald!

In which Harold Kleven's troubles end and Efi's are just beginning

E FI AND HARALD KLEVEN had turned heads when they moved into Colmar the previous spring. For one thing, the citizens regarded newcomers who were not merchants, minstrels, or tinkers with wary skepticism. For another, the couple were uncommonly attractive, and this was also highly suspect. Efi's hair fell in clouds of golden curls around her shoulders, and her figure remained healthy and plump when all around her shrank with hunger and grief. Harald was an Adonis, taller than average with bright blue eyes and a chin as firm and square as a blacksmith's anvil. The two of them strolling through the market or the church elicited grumbles of annoyance from their neighbors, followed by ambivalent neglect.

Had Efi and Harald arrived before the onset of the Great Pestilence, they might have been greeted with more hostility, but those who survived death in Colmar learned to be charitable (within reason), and above all, they did not have enough extra strength to care. The pestilence killed the strong and healthy workers alongside frail widows and children in equal measure, leaving the fields wild and unharvested due to a lack of workers. To care about a couple of beautiful strangers would mean diverting precious energy away from trying to survive. As soon as the new couple settled into their rented room near the city walls, Harald set about as a blacksmith's assistant, and Efi hired herself out to a wealthy burgher's wife to mind the children. Life in the city continued around them.

This was all the knowledge Gritta and Appel had when they arrived at the door of the deceased Harald Kleven, primped and ready to comfort the new widow. Old Hattie Jungerwald was already there speaking consolations to the girl, a wrinkled hand resting on Efi's back.

"Mostly it was Harald's idea," Efi sniffed, wiping her eyes on the half-finished kerchief she had been embroidering that morning. Gritta glanced at Appel and noticed the older woman's critical glare. The embroidery on the kerchief was crooked.

"He wanted to find a new place in a village where people would forget that he was the boy who accidentally burned Lord Dietrich's house to the ground. Get a fresh start, you know?"

Gritta cleared her throat gently, and the two women looked up at her.

"Your husband burned the castle of a lord?"

Efi sighed, then smiled slightly, her eyes clouding with memory. "Indeed, yes. He was trying to invent a way to shear lord Dietrich's sheep, you see, but not with shears. He had the idea to use a hot iron from the fire to burn the fleece from the sheep. Harald was a brilliant man. An inventor!"

"But..." Gritta could see Appel turning the problem over in her head. "You cannot burn wool. Not without trying your hardest. And what of the damage to the sheep?"

"And so Harald discovered." Efi blew her nose into her handkerchief. "But when he dropped the hot iron onto his breeches, my poor Harald did go up in flames, and when he was a'running about to put himself out, he thought to roll in the straw in the master's stables, to smother the flames, you know?"

Appel looked helplessly at Gritta, who shot back a look of bafflement.

"Well, that's the stupidest thing I ever heard, and make no mistake!" Gritta exclaimed.

Efi sobbed and dropped her face into her handkerchief. "That is what Lord Dietrich said, too!"

Next to her, Hattie Jungerwald nodded wearily. Efi had been carrying on all afternoon, but that was better than this absurd reminiscing. What could a nineteen-year-old woman have to reminisce about anyway? Hattie Jungerwald didn't know how old she was herself, but she only had three top teeth left, and that accounted for many years. She hated young people and their arrogance to possess memories and to reflect on those experiences, as if nineteen years of God-granted life was some sort of accomplishment.

The door creaked open and Efi jumped to her feet.

"Harald!" she cried dramatically, but it was only two more neighbor women who bore baskets of kuchen and fresh eggs.

"Oh, do stay," Efi sniffed. "I've made pottage."

The newcomers glanced at a small iron pot, which belched black smoke from the edge of the hearth. They began to edge back toward the door to make their escape, but Hattie Jungerwald arrived there first, shuffling as fast as her stiff joints would allow. Her relief at being able to leave was elevated by the fact that she didn't like Gritta and Appel. In Hattie Jungerwald's opinion, Gritta was a slovenly housewife, and Appel's pious churchmongering was merely a way to deflect attention from the fact that she was undoubtedly a witch.

For their part, Gritta and Appel looked at the pretty young widow in her throes of despair with a sort of rabid appetite for providing charity. It was, after all, something they had each become proficient at during the long years of the Great Pestilence. A look between the two of them confirmed their unspoken agreement. Efi's home was small but clean, and the board near her hearth was well stocked with turnips and grains, which the senseless girl didn't seem to know how to cook. They would have to move in for a few days.

"She's yours now," Hattie Jungerwald muttered on the way out. "And God grant you patience."

If Efi was a sentimental girl, she might have lamented the fact that she did not have her mother's bosom to cry on in this time of suffering. But she wasn't sentimental, although she was romantic in a superficial kind of way. When her father had complained that Harald had less sense than a nanny goat, Efi defended him passionately because that is what one must do to protect a handsome man. And Harald was lovely, with hair as thick and gold as a field of wheat before harvest, and a jutting trapezoid for a chin. God, she would miss that chin. They had only been married a short time and had already left one village of their own accord and been chased out of the other by Lord Dietrich when he discovered the smoldering remains of his castle. As she pondered the loss of her two previous homes and her young husband, she hardly noticed the two goodwives who had installed themselves in her home.

Gritta appeared to be enjoying her stay with the grieving widow. Occasionally, one or several of her many children would appear, dirty and shoeless, at Efi's door, begging their mother to resolve a quarrel or to provide instructions on how to care for their inebriated father. Gritta, having taken up a seat on a bench near the window, accepted their petitions like a queen listening to the complaints of her court. She crossed her ankles, issued decrees, and seemed in no hurry to return to her home, where the mending basket and washing tub waited for her.

Appel, her iron-gray hair tucked modestly underneath her chaste, white wimple, made herself comfortable on a stool near the light of the doorway and knitted placidly during the days. She maintained a benign smile and nodded with a gentle "yes dear" at anything that Efi said. Tied to her girdle was a string of polished wooden rosary beads that clacked whenever she moved. The old woman made certain that Harald had a good plot for burial, not inside the churchyard – for there was no room – but next to the wall, which the priests had blessed for burial overflow. Harald was stacked atop another poor soul who had perished only a few weeks earlier, but this was to be expected after the pestilence.

"Walls cannot contain God's sanctity," Appel told the young widow one day, doing her best to imbue her voice with wisdom. "And so Harald will have a little more blessing because he is so close to the church. And as you know, sometimes wild animals drag sticks and other things over the walls and leave them a'ground, which covers the grave with added holiness."

This was too much for Gritta, who dropped her embroidery in disgust.

"Appel, whatever are you talking about?"

Appel sniffed loudly, took Efi's hands in her own, and ignored her friend's remarks. "It is a pity that they had to place him atop old Herr Gilden, but there was so little space near the church, it was either that or bury him in the dooryard with the chickens.

He and Herr Gilden will keep each other company in purgatory, dear."

Appel was everything that Efi thought a mature widow ought to be – stately, demure, protective, and pious. Someday, she thought, after I have remarried and become widowed again, I shall be like this woman. I aspire to it. She glanced at Appel, and the old woman smiled, dipping her head like an agreeable monk.

None of the other goodwives in Les Tanneurs were willing to ensure that the young, witless widow of Harald Kleven was looked after, so Gritta and Appel stayed with Efi for two nights. But when it became apparent that the senseless girl was happy to take advantage of their generosity for as long as she could, they confronted her as she lay in bed, staring at the heavy beams of her rented home. In the apartments above, the sounds of a domestic dispute were filtering through the plaster.

"Come now, it is time for you to get up." Gritta peeled the woolen blanket back. "Keeping to your bed all day is a luxury only available to the childless, and I can't watch it any longer. Your husband may have died, but my hoe is missing, which will cause the starvation of my entire family, and I must return to my garden."

Efi shrieked as the chill morning air touched her naked body, and she threw a hand over her eyes. "Harald, my Harald!" she wailed.

"Aye, Harald doesn't have to listen to your carrying on any longer, the lucky man. Now go on, get yourself dressed and then fetch some water from the well. I'll bring the fire back to life."

Efi crossed her arms over her breasts, shivering as Gritta tossed a woolen chemise at her. "I am in mourning," she said, her voice breaking. "My Harald is gone, and so my heart with him!"

Gritta rolled her eyes and pulled the garment over Efi's head, threading her arms through the sleeves. "You lost your Harald at the perfect time – while you are both beautiful and before he became a drunk and a lech. Now go on, fetch that water. It's time for your resurgence."

"My resurgence?"

Gritta shooed Efi from the house, and she staggered into the gray light of the morning. A thick haze of smoke from chimneys of nearby houses hovered in the narrow lane, and a few small bats swooped through the dawn sky for their last meal before the sun fully rose. The air was cool but held a whiff of the heat which was bound to come later in the day. It did feel good to be outside again. When she returned from the well, a new fire crackled loudly in the hearth and the two older women were fastening their rough woolen cloaks around their shoulders.

"But where are you going? What about my resurgence?"

Appel patted Efi on the head. "You're off to a good start, my dear. Now you should go outside and feed your hens before they seek out the dooryard of another goodwife."

Efi's eyes brimmed with tears. "I am no longer a goodwife; I am a widow! A spent woman!"

Gritta and Appel both threw back their heads with surprisingly bawdy peals of laughter, and Gritta pulled the door open, stepping out into the lane. Although the sun had only barely risen, the residents of Colmar were now awake and bustling about their work. Women shuffled to and from the city well with water to fill their porridge pots, servants dragged small, two-wheeled carts loaded with goods for the markets, and children shouted and teased each other as they ran errands for their mothers. The growing din of life and commerce was a reassuring sound of lives returning to normal.

"Can you come back tomorrow? Can I stay with you?" Efi pleaded.

"Come visit us when you have lived a little longer," Appel laughed. She held out her arm for Gritta to take but jumped back suddenly as two elderly Dominicans from the nearby priory ran past, nearly knocking her to the ground. The men had their robes hitched up around their shins, and their cheeks were red and puffing with exertion. The three women watched this spectacle, mouths agape, and were about to continue their conversation when the friars presently raced back in the direction from which they had come, this time with Lord

Werner, the sheriff of Colmar, waddling behind them at his top speed.

"Well!" Gritta exclaimed. "I always suspected the sheriff of being a sinner, but he must have done something quite terrible to deserve such a summons!"

"No, my friend," Appel said slowly. "I think there is trouble afoot amongst the men of the priory."

Gritta rolled her eyes. "I just hope they're not trying to make bread again. Friar Ignatius' eyebrows are still gone."

Appel held her arm out again. "Well, shall we return to our homes, my dear?"

"We shall." Gritta took the proffered arm, and the two women began to stroll down the lane toward their own modest homes in the heart of Les Tanneurs.

"Wait!" Efi cried out. "What about my resurgence?"

"You are off to a good start, my dear!" Appel called back.

For a moment, Efi stood alone in the street. "Oh, my poor Harald!" She wailed, but no one came to comfort her. After years of pestilence and constant death, the period of mourning was short, and the need to return to everyday life urgent. She remained in front of her door for a moment until she was sure no one would come, then retreated into her empty, silent house.

Old priors and new friars

In which an arrangement is made between two factions

Father Konrad, the prior of the church of the Dominicans, sat at his table, his papery eyelids half-lowered. Steepling his fingers, he sized up the nervous Franciscan friar standing before him. The young man, Brother Wikerus was his name, had tucked his hands into the wide sleeves of his rough brown robe, but beneath the fabric his fingers fidgeted nervously. The prior glanced down at the parchment on his table and re-read the text.

"This is most irregular." Father Konrad shook his head, setting the parchment down and brushing aside the chips of broken wax from the document's seal.

The young friar bowed his head in respect. "Father Guillaume thought I could be of some assistance considering the current situation. Your..." He paused, searching for the right words. "Your predicament might require an unbiased party. And he also believes firmly in sharing amongst the brotherhoods."

"Indeed," the prior said slowly, "but I still cannot determine how Father Guillaume even knew that the items in the church were going missing. Only a few in this priory currently know about the thefts, and none of the burghers or lords were aware until I sent two brothers to fetch Sheriff Werner yesterday."

The friar looked down at his toes, and the prior sighed.

"Of course, I should have known. Our lord sheriff does sometimes forget to be discreet when he is in his cups."

The friar looked apologetic and uncomfortable. "Although I do not know the details, I believe that the good lord sheriff was, indeed, in the weinstube of Breisach and lamenting the loss of your sacred treasures. Word of your troubles reached Father Guillaume, and it is his wish to offer counsel and assistance, not to draw any attention to this most serious and appalling crime."

"Mm…" Father Konrad crossed his arms over his chest and narrowed his rheumy eyes. "And how does sending you here unannounced assist me in this time of trouble? Do you have a special skill for seeking out thieves?"

He scrutinized the young man for another moment. Brother Wikerus could not have been older than thirty. He was plump, shorter than most, and pale, with fine brown hair cropped close to his head except on the crown, which was shaved completely clean. He possessed unusually large eyes, which were dark blue and expressive, and he seemed conscious of them, for when the prior held his gaze, Brother Wikerus quickly averted his own, as if embarrassed. Again, the friar looked down at his feet, his fingers working furiously beneath the fabric of his sleeves.

"I am but a humble servant of God, my lord Prior, and I do not wish to elevate myself above any of my brothers at the priory. However, Father Guillaume instructed me to tell you that I have some skill at finding the truth of crimes such as these."

"Indeed, it says here that you apprehended a young noble who was planning to murder his father in order to take on his sire's estate."

The friar nodded, but he did not seem pleased to discuss the matter, and Father Konrad felt it best to change the subject.

"Do you read, Brother Wikerus?"

"Yes, my lord, although my writing is still in need of practice."

"What can you offer to me other than your skill in catching thieves? I have as many brothers and laymen as this priory and city can tolerate at the moment, and we cannot take on another unless there is a compelling reason. My own men here are capable of working with Sheriff Werner to catch the thief, for surely it will not be difficult to apprehend this person. All I need to do is post a guard in the nave of the church every day."

"As a Franciscan, I can be of service to the citizens of Colmar by offering counsel and support in these trying times."

The prior raised an eyebrow, and the friar continued quickly. "Although the Great Pestilence has passed and few fall ill these days from that evil affliction, there is always the Lord's work to be done in a city such as yours. Your Dominican brothers could surely use more help to serve the population. Allow me to minister to the community alongside them."

Father Konrad continued to assess the man, fingers pressing against each other, steepling and unsteepling. "Indeed, there is a place that we have a need in this city," he said slowly and then smiled. "I have decided that you may stay. In addition to your investigations with our sheriff, Lord Werner, you may also minister to the citizens in Les Tanneurs."

The friar paled slightly but didn't flinch. "The tannery district? Where the leather hides are cut and cured?"

"Yes. It is a part of the city where we do not have much influence. We've found the population there to be somewhat wayward and intractable. The tanners have a way of ruling themselves that is difficult for the law and the church to control. The pestilence hit that area of Colmar severely, and many widows in that neighborhood stubbornly refuse to remarry."

"Are the widows running the tanneries themselves in their husband's stead?"

"No indeed, for that work is not suitable for a woman. They make money by selling their vegetables in the markets or hawking their surplus ale. And they argue often. You will be much appreciated by all the good burghers and free men of this community if you can encourage more church attendance from them and gently persuade them to bind themselves in a holy union with new husbands, else this whole city will be overrun with quarrelsome and unchaste harpies."

"Convincing widows to remarry isn't exactly what I had in mi—"

"God calls us to do things we do not always wish, is that not right, Brother Wikerus? I can always send you back to Breisach if you think that is a better option. I am sure it smells more pleasant," the prior interrupted.

The young friar hung his head in apology, and the prior nodded.

"It is settled, then. Brother Marcus will show you to your quarters, and you can begin your ministrations tomorrow morning after Matins."

Friar Wikerus thanked Father Konrad and quietly left the room when it was clear that he had been dismissed. In the courtyard outside the prior's apartment, he leaned his back against the hot, rough stones of the wall and sighed heavily. He missed the fresh breezes and sweeping views in his hometown of Breisach but not much else. Here, where no one knew him, he could start fresh.

The Great Pestilence

In which the state of the world is explained

ON THE THIRD DAY of each week, Appel did her washing, and because she was a kind woman, she often did Gritta's as well. While most goodwives complained about their never-ending duties, Appel enjoyed them precisely because they were so dull. At least it was something to do – something to take her mind off of what the world had just survived. She took joy in every repetitive, annoying task because they reminded her that she still lived.

That anyone could feel happiness during the Great Pestilence and the years beyond was an indication that humankind had either remarkable resilience or an inability to comprehend the desperateness of their lives. For four years, the sickness ravaged every person in the land, from the beggars' settlements to the largest cities, and then it vanished, leaving the survivors shocked and bewildered. And yet, people in Colmar managed to find small ways to feel as if their lives were still normal. Throughout the terror, the heartache, the nights of heart-tearing screams when the pestilence was at its zenith, babies were born, couples fell in love, the sun rose and set, and the crops grew. Some lives carried on while others flicked out like candle flames.

At first, there were only rumors of a vile affliction that brought down men and women, children and the elderly, noble-born and commoner. Even the men of the church, who were the most chaste and contrite, could not pray protection over themselves sufficient to shield them from the fever, the violent shaking, and the appearance of the buboes and sores that preceded death.

Once the pestilence grasped ahold of a person, there were a few days of chill as the skin turned progressively darker and painful to the touch. Then the buboes would appear, raising the skin of the groin or the throat into angry, swollen masses of thick liquid. When they would burst, the smell was so foul that no one could remain nearby. Raving and then death followed quickly, as well as the spread of the affliction to other members of a family or an entire village. Not a single person in any town or city from Jerusalem to Bergen could say that they had not seen and experienced the effects of the pestilence, for it was greedy and insidious – almost like a living being.

The disease made saints and sinners out of everyone; some thought only God's hand of mercy could save them, and others became convinced that God's hand of vengeance knew no limits. Appel was more inclined to assume that a supreme show of repentance and worship would end their misery, and yet the years continued to drag with more death. She now felt sure that

God was just bored and that, like the great flood of Noah, the earth needed to be scoured of evil men and women.

The residents of Colmar had felt reasonably safe – after all, they were a pious community. They had even invited the Dominican holy men to return after Louis of Bavaria tossed them out. But when word arrived that Strassburg had succumbed to the pestilence, everyone knew that Colmar was not far behind. All people born of Strassburg and living in Colmar were kicked out, along with the Jews and the lepers, just to be safe. In Strassburg, they decided to kill off their Jews to ensure extra protection from God, and when the terror had gripped the citizens of Colmar sufficiently, they also put their Jewish citizens and neighbors to the sword. When this had no effect, they flagellated themselves, walking about the city and flailing their bodies with whips, mortifying their flesh into tattered strips of skin and muscle to appease God in heaven, who was clearly not satisfied with the souls of Jews. That their God was perhaps angered by the killing of Jews was something they preferred not to think about.

On Trench Lane, Gritta's husband Jorges took to drink in order to push away his terror of being overcome by the sour air that passed the pestilence from person to person. Gritta continued to have children as Appel buried hers, along with her grandson, husband, and the hired boy who helped with the tanning. The residents of Colmar pulled in on themselves and grieved privately. Where food could be found, they took it. Fields grew fallow, for the workers who typically tended and harvested the crops had all died. Goods did not move between cities because the merchants were dead or frightened of the hungry survivors whose desperation spurred them to commit robbery and murder on the roads. A generation of children grew up with a look of lost confusion in their eyes; the memory of tragedies that they had seen would never cease to haunt them.

Eventually, the pestilence removed itself to other cities and towns after slaking its appetite in Colmar. People slowly emerged from their cloud of grief and fear to try and build life and community again, though they suddenly did not know how. The old traditions were nothing more than hollow rituals. Clinging to the ways of life before the pestilence brought nostalgia but not comfort. The dead were still dead. The food was still scarce. The behavior of the weather was strange, and the presence of more foreigners from far-off places was unnerving. And so, every man and woman sought solace in their own way – at the bottom of a cup, in the arms of a lover, or on their knees in a cathedral.

As she dunked the laundry in the canal and rubbed it vigorously, Appel smiled to herself. For her, like all the residents of Colmar, "the world" consisted of the fertile black soil of the long and narrow Alsace valley, the smooth, slow waters of the Rhine, the dark green shoulders of the nearby mountains, and the routine of daily life. There was comfort in the mundane tasks, like laundering the soiled clothing, for all who survived the pestilence knew that it was a privilege to become bored of their lives and work, since they were the few remaining who still possessed these things.

It was in this world that Gritta, Appel, and Efi would soon realize they had the chance to take hold of their fortunes, for better or for worse.

Hattie Jungerwald

In which a disturbance takes place in the night

G RITTA SAT STRAIGHT UP from where she slept, surrounded by seven of her eight children who still lived in the house. Underneath her blanket, the straw mattress shifted and crackled, inciting a series of snorts and groans from the young bodies arrayed around her. Nearby, Jorges was sprawled on his bench, snoring. But it wasn't Jorges' nightly ululations that had pulled her from sleep; it was a high-pitched shriek coming from outside the shutters.

Immediately, Gritta felt her limbs begin to quake. For years, screams could be heard ringing out in the night. It wasn't death that caused her neighbors to cry out but the discovery of fever or buboes on themselves or their loved ones. The end always came with whimpering and shivers, but the revelation of the disease brought about paroxysms of uncontrolled terror. Some even brought about their own deaths with poison or a noose to spare themselves the agony of the pestilence.

Gritta felt the old fear once again.

For a moment, the little square in Les Tanneurs echoed with the yell and fell silent, and then another followed – a different voice this time, but also that of a woman, and Gritta deflated with relief. It was only Hattie Jungerwald, the elderly widow who lived at the far end of the tannery district. Her husband, deceased in the pestilence, had collected the urine and feces – human and animal – that softened the hides before the tanner's apprentices could wash, dye, and scrape them so they could be turned into leather for shoes and saddles. Each morning, the old man staggered from house to house with his decrepit mule and cart, a large, sloshing barrel lashed to the sideboards, and collected the contents of the chamber pots. Now that he was dead, Hattie labored with the cart alone, unable to afford a mule or an ox, until the strain bent her back and twisted her legs.

Gritta pulled the shutter open and peered outside. In the moonlight, Hattie stood in a pale, ankle-length chemise with dark embroidery along the hem, her downy white hair uncovered and floating around her face, and pointed a bony finger at another figure in the street. Frau Widmer, the other source of the noise, stood across the trench at a distance.

"Bitch!" Hattie screamed. "Stay away from my house while I sleep, or I will have you dragged to the pillory!"

Frau Widmer drew herself up, and Gritta could see the woman's chest fill with air as she prepared her counterattack.

"Proof! I have proof!" Frau Widmer screamed.

"You have no proof. None at all, but I have proof that you are a peeper. Go around looking in the windows of someone else's house, will you!"

"And you're a thief!"

"I am a good Christian woman!" Hattie shrieked and rushed at Frau Widmer, fingers bent into claws and ready to slash at her accuser's face.

This would never do. Gritta staggered around in the dark of her house, searching for her shawl, and was about to run out the door to break up the fighting when Girard, the night watchman, casually strolled over to the two women and pushed them apart. The three spoke in reasonable tones for a moment, and Gritta had to strain her ears to hear their conversation.

"Now go home, both of you," Girard said. "For shame! Good, pious women do not fight in the streets in naught else but their underclothes! I shall have the sheriff punish the both of you for public indecency if you don't go inside at once and go to sleep."

The two women cast malevolent glares at one another and shuffled off to their homes. Gritta yawned wide and retreated to the darkness of her house and the warm pile of sleeping bodies. Hattie and Frau Widmer had hated each other for as long as anyone could remember. There was always a disagreement between the two of them, although not usually at this hour. Doubtless, she would hear all about it in the morning when Hattie came around with her barrel for the chamber pot, which, since Jorges had been drinking ale this night, was brimful already.

As she carefully settled back onto her mattress between her children, she heard a snort and a thud as Jorges rolled off his bench and fell to the floor without waking.

Gritta cursed Hattie Jungerwald and Frau Widmer the following morning as she toiled through her chores in a fog of exhaustion. Several of her children strolled out of the house after their morning pottage, hopefully to earn money or find spouses for themselves. The twins, Anstett and Mattheus, had inflated a pig's bladder and made a ball, which they threw against the wall of the house, bringing down little showers of flaking plaster from the ceiling. On the floor, baby Wina squalled, swinging her plump fists in angry protest because Gritta had removed several stones and a beetle from the girl's mouth. Gritta sighed and sat down – a rarity during the day, when she was always on her feet.

"Just you go ahead and yell at me, child. Someday when I'm old and daft, I'll yell at you, just like our aged neighbor last night." She paused as an enormous yawn split her face, and in that pause, there was a knock at the door.

A friar stood there, dressed in a rough brown robe and cowl. Instead of a nicely braided girdle, like the Dominicans, he wore a hemp rope about his waist, but Gritta knew he was a friar by his tonsure, the circle of bare, shaved skin on the crown of his head.

"Greetings, Friar. What brings you to my door?" She curtseyed, as was proper.

"Greetings, goodwife Gritta. I wish to introduce myself. I am Friar Wikerus, and I've come to offer comfort to the residents of Les Tanneurs during this time of challenge."

"What challenge?" A voice behind them spoke, and the friar turned around. Efi stood outside, her head cocked to one side, blonde curls escaping her wimple. This was the first day Gritta had seen the girl venture from her house since Harald's death.

"Well then, you must be Harald Kleven's widow. Father Konrad, the prior of the Church of the Dominicans informed me of your recent tragedy. My apologies for not visiting you upon your widowhood, but I was only just given my orders for Colmar. I am Friar Wikerus, recently arrived from Breisach."

Efi's eyes clouded with tears at the mention of her husband's name, and Gritta crossed her arms, eyeing the friar sourly.

"Well, now you've set her crying again. We are busy, Friar Wikerus. If you will excuse us, I am sure that there are many who require your services. Might I suggest the Widmers? Surely Frau Widmer will want prayer after she spent the night waking all the lane with her yelling."

"Indeed, my apologies for interrupting your work and causing distress. I am positioned with the Dominicans if you require comfort for your grief, though they are not my order."

"Grief, Friar Wikerus? The pestilence is gone from Colmar, and hopefully also from the rest of God's kingdom as well."

Friar Wikerus blinked at them for a moment, and then his mouth opened in surprise.

"Then you have not heard?"

"Heard what?"

"Your neighbor, Hattie Jungerwald, was found dead this morning in her bed."

Misunderstandings

In which the efficacy of cabbages against overheated bosoms is proved

N EWLY WIDOWED EFI STOOD alone and sniffling outside the door of Frau Appel's house, waiting for someone to discover her distress. Inside, she could hear Appel and Gritta gossiping through the thin wattle and daub walls. She sobbed a little louder, but the two women were cackling like broody hens, drowning out her carefully planned tears. Only that morning, the widow Jungerwald had been discovered dead in her bed, which took attention away from Efi's misfortunes. The honey cakes had stopped arriving, the offers of help with the chores had dried up, and no one visited anymore. Worst of all, she was lonely.

"Ohhh…" Efi moaned. "Whatever will I do now?"

More laughter from inside. Efi stomped her foot. This indifference to her grief was unacceptable. She set her shoulder against the front door and found the two of them inside, sitting on the floor with legs sprawled and skirts hitched up to their waists. Each woman had a small clay jug next to her.

"Oh my," Efi stuttered, blushing at their uncouth postures and the thick fumes of wine rising from their bodies. "I will come back later." She backed away to leave, but Appel stood.

"Join us, my dear. We're coolin' our legs and having a bit of a gab. Come now, the heat's insufferable, but there's a nice draft over here near the hearth."

Efi walked inside and sat primly on the edge of a bench near the dark hearth. Sure enough, a cool breeze whistled from the chimney and into the room, smelling faintly of creosote and burned meat. Gritta sighed from her position in front of the dark hearth, fanning herself with a large cabbage leaf.

"Another person in this room is just adding more heat!" She stuffed the cabbage leaf down the front of her dress. When she saw Efi's eyes widen, Gritta shrugged. "The leaves keep my dugs cool. You should try it."

Appel tossed a cabbage, which Efi caught awkwardly, then she leaned forward, a matronly smile on her face.

"Go on, Efi dear, a little cabbage on the bosom does a woman wonders."

Efi clutched the head of cabbage and considered all the ways she might escape. She came here seeking comfort and a bit of sympathy, but these women were mad.

"Do not speak of bosoms, Appel! Not while Hattie's corpse is still cooling in the cellar beneath the cloisters!" Gritta stabbed the air with a defiant finger.

"W-was it the pestilence?" Efi whispered, and the two women turned a sympathetic eye to her.

"No," Appel said. "Hattie was old. Old people die, and if they are fortunate enough to die in their sleep, then God must truly love them."

Gritta snorted. "She looked well enough last night when she was hollering in the square. Her voice was strong, and her arm too, for I saw her preparing to strike Frau Widmer across the face."

"True enough. Hattie Jungerwald was hearty, I'll give her that." Appel took a deep drink from her jug. "Sometimes the lord God works in ways unfathomable."

"I think it is perfectly fathomable to assume that Frau Widmer finally did what we all knew she would do someday and killed Hattie." Gritta paused to belch loudly. "And I will wager the rest of this fine ale in my jug that she probably did it by strangling Hattie with the very chemise she accused the old crone of stealing."

"Murder?" Efi's eyes were wide, and she clutched her cabbage to her chest.

"Nonsense!" Appel said quickly. "We don't have murderers here in Colmar. Now, I wouldn't put anything past those heathens in Mulhouse."

"Hattie was in fine form last night," Gritta said emphatically. "She didn't die of no natural causes."

"What reason would anyone, other than Frau Widmer, have to kill old Hattie? There's no sense in it."

"Could have been a Jew," Gritta said, and quickly looked over her shoulder.

"I doubt it. There are no Jews left living in Colmar."

For a moment, the two women were silent as they recalled the nights of chanting mobs and burning bodies, and the rows of houses in the Jewish quarter whose shuttered windows were now as lifeless as their former owners. A strange, uncomfortable feeling crept up on them whenever they remembered the executions; guilt.

"A foreigner, then?" Efi asked. "A Dane?"

"You are as foreign as visitors get here, Efi," Gritta smirked.

"That new friar – Wikerus, he calls himself – asked me to help prepare the body," Appel grumbled. "As if I want to tend to the dead. He thinks I am as old and frail as Hattie was!"

"Will he pay you?" Gritta asked.

"I doubt it."

"Well, if he would pay, I would take your place." Gritta heaved a great sigh, her shoulders slumping slightly. Appel and Efi both looked at her, and she gave them an apologetic smile.

"He's gone and done it. Jorges fell into the manure pit at Lord Frider's winter estate and hurt his arm while he helped the lord's men to sweeten the fields, and only two days after the sheriff put him in the pillory for drunkenness! I'm ruined. My children and I shall all starve." She reached down to her jug and swigged from it unsteadily. "And without my hoe, I will be plowing my garden with my own hands come spring."

"You will find your hoe, Gritta." Appel placed a hand on her friend's knee.

"My papi always said Jorges was as ugly as a mule and twice as unlucky. But when we wed, I was pregnant with my Lisette, and I still thought well of Jorges back then." She looked down the barrel of her jug for a moment, eyes clouded with memory, then passed it up to Efi.

"Is there not a way that you can earn some money?" Appel asked, tipping back her own jug.

"Excuse me," Efi said timidly as she slid from her bench seat and onto the floor in front of the hearth, which was cooler and more comfortable. "But doesn't the bishop in Strassburg say that woe and suffering shall come upon a woman found in a state of drunkenness?"

Appel leveled the younger woman with a flat stare and arched a condescending eyebrow. "Child, this golden ale was given by God, and he loves me as he loves you. I wouldn't want to offend his good grace by turning up my nose at his bounty. The bishop takes plenty o' his own wine at meals, too."

"Amen," Gritta hiccoughed.

Appel returned her attention to Gritta, whose eyelids were beginning to slip downwards.

"Gritta! My dear, you must find work. Efi, you too, else you may both be turned out of your homes and sent to live with the nuns."

Efi and Gritta both shuddered.

"Could you apply to become a washerwoman at the castle?" Appel turned to her neighbor.

"No indeed, I already asked. The castle is full up on washerwomen, and the washerwomen are full up on Lord Frider's bastards – every one of them with a pregnant belly the size of a waterskin." Gritta drank again.

"Sell your vegetables in the market."

"My children eat everything I grow, includin' the weeds."

"Well, that explains a lot," Appel said under her breath.

Gritta stared dully into the dark hearth. "And if I cannot find my missing hoe to turn the earth come spring, I won't even be able to grow weeds for them."

"How does one lose a hoe, Gritta? It is a large tool."

"Jorges insisted that he didn't take it to Lord Frider's estate, and I can't prove that my useless son Lonel sold it, although he probably did. That child will end up hanging from a noose someday."

"Haven't you a sharpened stick to use instead?"

"Of course I can sharpen a stick, but I own a hoe and I prefer to use it. It was a wedding gift from Jorges."

"Ah yes." Appel rolled her eyes. "Sentimental as always, your Jorges."

"We could compose sonnets and sing," Efi suggested. "People in the square would give us money, and perhaps we would even be invited to—"

Gritta leaned over and gave the back of Efi's blonde head a sound slap. "Don't be daft. You're not as fair as you think, and I doubt you're half as talented."

Efi rubbed her head, ready to mount a fiery counterattack, but Appel stood suddenly, holding her small ale jug up to the shaft of light that struck a dusty beam through the window's open shutters.

"Of course. Of course!"

Gritta and Efi exchanged a confused glance.

"Gritta, where did this ale come from?"

"I don't know, Appel – it's your ale."

"Oh, right you are. I purchased it in the market, doled out in pittances by a stingy brewster from Vogelgrun. No one else is selling ale right now on account of there not being enough brewsters after the pestilence, and he sells it on behalf of the monks. The price is high because the monks take most of the profit."

"You could just buy it directly from the priory," Efi suggested, but Appel shook her head.

"Too expensive, and besides, it's too strong. They make the ale for their tastes and prefer to be as inebriated as possible. How else could they spend so much time in each other's company without going mad?"

"Isn't that what we're doing right now? Getting as inebriated as possible?" Efi asked. She had stealthily hitched her skirts to her waist like Appel and Gritta and was luxuriating in the sensation of free limbs and a cool breeze on her knees.

Now Gritta was also standing. "We can brew ale! We can brew ale and sell it for less than the monks! We'll undercut those pious dullards and take all their customers!"

Appel shot Gritta a scandalized look, but she quickly recovered.

"I, of course, do not require the income, but I shall consult. After all, I brewed for my family, and there were those who said my red barley wine was as fine as anything the monks made. I will share my knowledge with you."

Gritta rolled her eyes. "If you ain't helping with the labor, you ain't getting any of the profits, Appel. Come now, your husband is dead. Surely you need the money."

"I do not."

"Then where are you getting money?" Efi asked, and Appel balled her fists, readying herself for a fight. Before the women could come to blows, a knock at the door made all three of them jump. Gritta pulled the wilted cabbage leaves from her dress and tossed them into the washbasin, and Appel yanked the hem of her skirts down to her ankles. Efi ran to open the door and found the young Franciscan friar standing there. He smiled genially, bowing his tonsured head with the appropriate amount of sagacity for a man of God.

"Friar Wikerus!"

The smile froze on Friar Wikerus's face for a moment as he took in the leaking jug of ale and limp cabbage leaves protruding from the top of Efi's dress.

"Hello, Frau Efi. I am here to speak with Frau Appel."

Efi stood aside to let him in, but the friar smiled again. "I shall speak with her outside the house, if you please."

Having relocated herself to her bench, Appel stood and bowed as demurely as she could on her unsteady legs. "This is an honor, Friar, but I assure you, I need no assistance. Many of the less fortunate in our quarter would benefit from your services far more than I."

"Nevertheless, I should like to sit in your garden. The evening is warm, and the light has not yet faded."

Appel lifted her chin, straightened her skirts, and walked erect and stately into the small yard behind her house, seating herself on a large stone. Gritta followed on wobbly legs, and Friar Wikerus smiled again.

"Blessings upon you, goodwife Gritta. I am sure your children will require their evening meal from you soon. Give them my greetings."

Gritta's lip curled, but she plucked at Efi's sleeve.

"Come, girl. We're not wanted."

As they climbed the small stile in the stone wall that protected Appel's garden, Friar Wikerus sat on a tree stump and rested his elbows on his knees.

"Well," they heard him say as they slowly walked away. "I have been taking confession from several men on the city council today, and I have a few questions to ask you, Frau Appel."

"By God's nostrils"

In which Colmar gains three new alewives

THE NEXT DAY, EFI appeared at Appel's doorstep again, and this time she was crying with complete sincerity. Appel ushered her inside, of course. The child was about as intelligent as a lost hen, but she cried so prettily, and besides, she had no people.

Well, what was Appel supposed to do? This girl needed help. She needed to find a husband or a nunnery, or she could become problematic, and after her little "discussion" with Friar Wikerus, Appel knew that the eyes of the church would be on all three of them. The mere thought of that talk with the Franciscan yesterday caused Appel to look over her shoulder nervously. It was a surprise to learn that Colmar had so many men who preferred to keep their consciences clear.

Between sniffles and choking sobs, Efi explained that she was about to be turned out from her home.

"I don't know what to do, Frau Appel," she wailed. "For I have no skill at needlework or washing linens, and if I cannot find a man to marry me soon, I shall have to sell the only thing I have." She turned her face away dramatically. "My body."

"No," Appel said quickly, "don't do that."

"Aye," a voice interrupted them as Gritta let herself in. "For we decided already: we shall brew. And, my dears, we must act now. Herr Geld, the chief brewster in Vogelgrun, has died. I heard it this morning from Karl Gastwirt, the innkeeper. No one in Colmar brews large enough quantities for Karl's customers, and he hasn't the time and the patience to make it himself. The man is beside himself with worry. There is now no source of ale in the city other than what our own goodwives concoct in their stables. We will never have another chance like this."

"Herr Geld died?" Efi cried. "For shame! And when so many have already succumbed to the pestilence!"

"How did Herr Geld die?" Appel asked.

"Something to do with a funnel and an ox prod."

Appel made an "ah" expression but decided not to ask further questions. She cleared her throat. "Well, it seems I shall also need a source of coin after all."

Gritta raised an eyebrow. "Your conversation with Friar Wikerus did not go well, then?"

Appel ignored the remark. "Let us brew. I have the largest house and the freshest water, so we can set up our kettles here. Do either of you have grain stores?"

Gritta shook her head. "Naught but for seed. My cursed children insist that they must eat to live, and it is the grain they eat."

"I have some barley seed," Efi volunteered. "It was Harald's wish that we start our own allotment next year. He saved grain."

"Good. Perhaps Harald's brain wasn't entirely stuffed with burnt wool and turnips, then. Because Gritta and I live upstream, the water shall come from our section of the canal, so our ale isn't befouled. Do either of you have a tub for the mash?"

"Aye," Gritta grunted. "One tub, and I may be able to convince my boy Noe to build me another, as he's apprenticing with the cooper behind the church of Saint Martin. Mine will do fine, except on Fridays when we use it for the weekly bathing."

Efi's forehead was wrinkled in thought. "Who would even buy this ale? After all, I know of hardly anyone who drinks ale anyhow. We drank far more in Kleve, where I am from, but here in Colmar, everyone is wild for wine."

"Not when workin' the fields. Not for the babes with their morning bread. We can't all have wine," Gritta replied.

"But won't every goodwife in the city begin to brew since there is now no place to buy ale? We will have competition."

For a moment, all three of them lapsed into quiet thought. Then Appel cleared her throat.

"Gritta, I think you should ask Noe to make some more barrels and tubs. If we can brew enough ale, the goodwives of

Colmar won't attempt to make their own. They don't have the time anyhow. They would much rather buy."

Gritta nodded her head firmly. "Then it is settled. We are alewives now, and by God's nostrils, we shall brew the finest ale in Colmar!"

Decisions made under duress often exclude important details. In this case, that detail was the rapidly decomposing corpse of Hattie Jungerwald.

Appel remembered that she had promised Friar Wikerus to help prepare the body for its pauper's burial, which dampened her enthusiasm for brewing. She sighed and untied her apron.

"We have much work to do, but first I must complete this service for my old neighbor. It's a pity she's not here, for Hattie did know the best way to brew a three-day yarrow ale."

Gritta and Efi promised to clean up, giving Appel sympathetic looks as she trudged out the door to her unpleasant task, and they were surprised when she came running back only a short time later.

"Appel, you look as if you've seen the dead come back to life. Hattie didn't jump at you, did she?" Gritta exclaimed.

Appel was panting so forcefully from the run home that she could hardly stutter out a response.

"Girls, Hattie didn't die peacefully in her sleep. It is as you said, Gritta dear. She was murdered!"

"What?!" Gritta and Efi responded in unison, and Appel nodded her head vigorously.

"When I undressed her to prepare the body with the nuns, what do you think I saw? The skin around her throat was purple with bruises. And what is more, I clearly saw the signs of a man's fingers on her throat. Someone strangled her, and with his own hands!"

"Heavens!" Efi cried out.

"I knew it!" Gritta crowed triumphantly. "I knew that old hen was too cross and vigorous to simply drop dead in her house. She was healthy enough to split logs with her fingernails if she wanted."

"Why would someone kill an old woman in her sleep?" Efi cried out, hands clasped to her chest.

Appel looked darkly at both women. "I do not know, but whoever did it has not been brought to justice. The murderer is still roaming Colmar, unless he has fled. Surely we would have heard some news about it if Sheriff Werner had caught someone a'muderin' in our fair city."

The women looked at each other, and in that silence, they heard the sound of a man stifling a sneeze. Efi tiptoed to the door and pulled it open. Sheriff Werner himself stood there, wiping his nose and blushing furiously.

"Sheriff, oh thank the saints that you are here." Efi tugged at the man's sleeve, dragging him over the threshold. "Did you hear our conversation? You must go see the body of Hattie Jungerwald at once!"

"It is urgent, Sheriff! We think she was murdered!" Gritta yelled.

Sheriff Werner's eyebrows shot upwards. "And why do you think she was murdered, Frau Gritta?"

Appel stepped forward. "She was strangled, my lord. Saw the murderer's fingerprints on the flesh of her throat with my own eyes, I did."

Sheriff Werner frowned. "The nuns did not tell me of this."

"Did you not see the body yourself, Sheriff?"

"Indeed not. Preparing the body of a dead woman is not my responsibility. And she is an old woman besides. Very likely that the lord God took her soul as she slept."

"But—"

"This is nonsense. We do not have murderers in Colmar. A straight and true city this is. Why, did you know that the great Charlemagne himself used to reside in our little city? Imagine that!"

"But, my lord, if you would only listen to what Frau Appel has to say—" Gritta began, but the sheriff merely increased the strength of his voice and spoke over her.

"And as you are aware, there is ample reason to believe that I am a descendant of his. Charlemagne, that is. Improperly recorded, of course, for that was a thousand years ago." Sheriff Werner scratched his chin, for a moment looking as if he intended to find the scribe responsible for improperly recording his family's storied ancestry. "I ought to have that little oversight corrected."

"But, my lord—"

Sheriff Werner cut Appel off with a wave of his hand and turned to Gritta.

"Well, that is not my business here today. Frau Gritta, I have come because we've had to put Jorges in the pillory for drunkenness again, and I'll take three coppers from you to let him out."

Gritta paled. "Three coppers? I haven't three coppers today. Jorges hasn't worked because of his arm."

"Well, that is the price to release a man early. If you don't pay, he'll stay there until tomorrow."

Gritta's expression darkened. "Then let him stay in the pillory. Perhaps he will sober long enough to remember what happened to my missing hoe. Now, Sheriff, will you investigate Hattie Jungerwald's death? We may have a murderer roaming the streets of Colmar!"

The sheriff snorted and folded his hands over his ample midsection – a reliable sign that he was about to pontificate. "And we also have a heathen who is stealing directly from God's house, and I assure you, this is a far more heinous crime than dispatching a belligerent old woman."

When Sheriff Werner noticed the shocked expression on the women's faces, he recalled that he had promised the prior of the Dominicans that he would not breathe a word of the church thefts to a soul. It was a promise which he had already broken at least twice. It would take a full confession to atone for his lack of discretion. He shifted his weight uncomfortably from foot to foot.

"Well, I will be off. Gritta, you know where to find your husband when you're ready for him."

Efi had less grain than they were led to believe, so Gritta skimmed a bit from the porridge pot each morning, and Appel ate leeks and onions for days instead of barley, which gave her the very devil's breath. Between the three of them, they scraped together a peck of cracked wheat kernels, a handful of stale oats, and some slightly soggy barley. It smelled suspicious, but it was enough grain to start their work.

Appel insisted on secrecy. It was imperative, she said, that no one have an opportunity to sabotage their work. They made a small batch at first – grain, water, a bit of honey, and some bread mash. Their first task was to malt the grain by drying it over a flame, which they did with more enthusiasm than necessary, resulting in a brew that, as Gritta put it, "tasted like someone pissed in the ash pit of hell."

On their second try, Gritta discovered a small sack of barley in her son Lonel's trunk – probably stolen from the market – which she contributed to the cause. They took more care with the malt, pouring the golden grain directly into Appel's iron pot, which had been heating gently over the fire, and immediately stifled the coals with a layer of sand to keep the temperature consistent and mild. Then they took turns stirring the barley constantly with a great wooden spoon, which made their arms ache and caused beads of sweat to rise upon their brows. They then scoured the pot and filled it with fresh water. Once they brought that to a boil, the malt was poured in, only to be scooped out again before it could add too much bitterness to the brew. They were out of honey, so Efi suggested a bit of beetroot for sweetness, which turned the mixture a frightful color.

After they allowed the brew to sit, covered with a cloth, for two days, they all gathered at Appel's house one crisp, late summer morning to taste the results.

"You're the oldest, Appel dear. You try it first," Gritta urged.

"Well, it was mostly my grain used," Efi muttered under her breath, but the older women ignored her remarks. Appel smiled graciously and, with much gravitas, took a sip from her dipper.

"Well?" Efi and Gritta asked in unison.

"It's...foul," Appel gagged, then she ran to the washbasin in the corner and tipped it into her mouth, gargling for a moment before spitting the pinkish brew out the window.

Gritta slumped into her chair. "Two batches of ale wasted, all the malt burned, and no more grain for our bellies, neither."

"Had you listened to my advice, the brew would be milder," Efi grumbled, still in a foul humor from Gritta and Appel's chastisement.

"Adding sheep's kidneys will not make the brew milder, you silly child." Gritta waved her away, and Appel heaved a sigh.

"But kidneys are a sweet meat." Efi crossed her arms and turned her back to them. "There's sense in it."

More days passed. The brew's taste gradually improved so the women could swallow it without gagging, but it spoiled within a day or two, and nothing they tried would preserve it. Gritta tried adding salt, reasoning that when she used salt to cure fish and cabbage, the spoil stayed away. Efi insisted on adding a shed snakeskin, since it preserved the animal from the elements, but although it didn't alter the taste, none of the women could stomach the thought of drinking a brew made with a dead skin. Appel incanted over the brew pot and insisted on profound, monastic silence during the fermentation, preferring to rely on divine intervention to ensure the freshest quality. This gave Gritta an uncomfortable prickle of recollection in the far reaches of her memory. There were rumors about Appel's past as a woman whose herb tonics and unusual prayers had uncanny results. She swept these thoughts from her mind, however. Appel was as dear to Gritta as an overbearing older sister. If her friend said she wasn't a witch, then Gritta believed her.

Despite their innovations, the ale always tasted the same, which the women agreed was "fine." Still, they only had enough for themselves and Gritta's children, who complained bitterly that their weak ale with supper smelt of burned pottage and garden soil.

During their labors, the three women mused about the death of old Hattie, who now lay under an unmarked mound of dirt near the church. Like Harald, her body was atop another to save space.

Appel took care to clean Hattie's mound of twigs and leaves every Lord's Day, and Gritta even took a moment to lay a wreath of posies on it. Heavy rainstorms hammered the valley, flattening the grain crops and Hattie's mound, diminishing evidence that she had walked the earth, until she was nothing more than a little bump of soil and a wilted wreath of flowers. There was no interest, it seemed, in investigating the untimely demise of an old widow.

Investigations

In which a meal of venison over bread enables a theft

FRIAR WIKERUS STARED OPENMOUTHED at the bare altar while the old Dominican friar near him paced and wrung his parchment-white hands in agitation.

"I just needed to use the privy, Brother Wikerus. I only went out for a moment to relieve myself as God requires it, and when I returned, lo! Our gold and even the altar cloth were thieved!"

Wikerus was baffled. He had seen that gold on this very altar during his prayers at Prime.

"But the privy is not far from here, Brother Ignatius! And how long does it take a man to make water, especially when he knows he is to stand guard?"

Brother Ignatius adjusted his black robe with dignity. "I weren't makin' no water, and I'm an old man, Brother Wikerus. Whenever the cook serves venison over bread for the evening meal, it does cause my bowels to slow, and as you know—"

"Never mind, Brother Ignatius. Your meaning is clear. So you were gone for some time."

"More time than it takes to walk thrice around the courtyard, I reckon. Mind you, venison over bread is quite nice, but this time the bread was most dry. Most dry indeed."

Friar Wikerus scowled and squatted down on the ground near the altar. It was perfectly clean. Too clean.

"Brother Ignatius, when was this floor last washed?"

"Well, there was the old woman who came to clean the floors as I discovered the missing items. She does a fine job of sweeping up."

"And you let her sweep up after a theft had occurred in our own nave?" Friar Wikerus kept his voice calm, though he wanted to yell at the old monk before him.

"Didn't want to take the woman from her work. She is a widow, you know."

"Why did you not immediately call for help, allowing no other person into the nave?"

"You never gave such instructions, Brother Wikerus," Brother Ignatius crossed his arms indignantly. "And Sheriff Werner did come to help. He was nearby when the crime took place, as was the old woman."

Wikerus turned sharply to the old man. "Sheriff Werner was here? Why?"

"Had business with the prior, he did. He was leaving through the courtyard when he heard my cries."

"Was the floor clean when he came in?"

"Well, let's see then." Brother Ignatius rubbed at the shorn patch of skin on the top of his skull. "No, the old woman came in to clean the floors while the sheriff inspected the altar."

This was maddening. Why would the sheriff allow someone to clean the floors immediately after a theft? Why had the sheriff not come directly to Friar Wikerus when he heard of the thefts? Surely the prior must have told the man that Wikerus was the ecclesiastical investigator. He did not want the nobility involved in the investigations of the church.

"I will go to the prior. Hopefully, the sheriff is still there, reporting on what he found in the nave."

Without waiting for a reply from Brother Ignatius, Friar Wikerus spun and trotted out of the church and across the courtyard, which was now quite dark. A single lamp hanging from a hook over the prior's lintel flickered and illuminated the heavy iron bolt of the door. Friar Wikerus pushed this open and found Father Konrad inside, head stooped in prayer over his folded hands. Friar Wikerus stopped abruptly and bowed, muttering a prayer of supplication and apology to the Lord for allowing the holy items of the church to disappear.

When he had finished praying, the prior raised his eyes and scowled.

"Well, Brother Wikerus?"

Wikerus dropped to one knee. "I am as grieved as you are, my lord. But please do not blame Brother Ignatius. He was tending to the call of nature when the crime occurred, and there was nothing that he could have done. Next time I shall set two guards instead of one."

"Whatever are you talking about?"

"D-did Sheriff Werner not come to tell you?" Friar Wikerus stuttered in amazement. "Not even after it happened?"

"After what happened?"

"The gilt cross set with purple rubies was stolen from the church altar this very evening."

"What?" Father Konrad leaped to his feet and roared. "How could you let this happen?"

"I...it was...that is to say, I thought Sheriff Werner would have mentioned it to you."

"It is not Sheriff Werner's job to tell me of these things and to prevent them; it is yours!"

"Yes, my lord." Friar Wikerus bowed his head again quickly and jumped to his feet. "I shall go into town immediately after prayers at Prime and make inquiries."

The worth of an industrious woman

In which the alewives gain a surprising patron

T HE STUBBORNLY HOT SUMMER gave way so suddenly to autumn that there was hardly enough time to pick the pears from the trees and settle the animals indoors. The shorn barley fields were bristly with stubble when an early and unexpected first frost arrived. Gritta moved her hens and the one scrawny goat into a partitioned corner of the house to exchange a little body heat. Efi constantly complained about the effect of the dry, cold air on her complexion, and Appel dragged her straw-stuffed mattress downstairs to be near the warmth of the fire and the bubbling vats of mash.

The seasons may have changed, but the quality of the ale remained mediocre.

"Efi, you'll take this sieve and strain the mash today." Appel handed the girl a mesh of finely woven willow twigs as she prepared to scrub the fermenting tub one morning. They had been working at the ale since the first cock crowed, and as their stomachs growled, their patience waned.

"But my hands!"

"The mash leavings are good for your hands. Go on now."
Appel patted the young woman on her curly blonde head, then
joined Gritta in front of the hearth. Gritta had a handful of
hazelnuts that she cracked between two stones like a squirrel,
tossing the empty shells into the fire.

"You know, Gritta dear, I have been thinking about the
problem of selling this ale."

"Is there a problem?"

"Well, I'm a tanner's widow, and Efi's Harald was a
blacksmith's assistant. We can carry on with the work of our late
husbands, but since neither was a brewster, we are not allowed
such a quantity of ale. That leaves you, but the word around the
city is that the bishop in Strassburg did preach against women
selling wares at all."

"Well, let them preach. We're in Colmar, not Strassburg."

"Just so. I would not wish to go against the word of a bishop."

"Appel, you can fool everyone else into thinking that you are
a godly woman, but I know better. Just lie to the bishop."

Appel stood and straightened her skirts, leveling Gritta with
a haughty glare. "Well, at least I am trying to do what is right in
the eyes of God."

"God's eyes are rolling in his head right now."

The door was closed, but the shutters remained open to let
in a bit of light. Outside Appel's house was a clear view down
Trench Lane to Hattie Jungerwald's small, shabby house, and
the women could see porters moving benches and tables inside

to fit a new resident. Appel, Gritta, and Efi all watched in silence for a moment.

"Who do you think it could have been, Appel?" Gritta whispered. "Hattie's been in her grave for more than a fortnight now, yet no one cares that she was murdered."

Appel shook her head and pressed her lips into a thin line. "Whoever they are, God knows what they've done."

The scrawny figure of Frau Widmer appeared in the lane, and she poked her birdlike face inside Hattie's doorway as she complained to the workers about the noise. Appel clucked her tongue sharply.

"Frau Widmer was the last person to speak to Hattie; foul words they were, too."

"I still think old Widmer did Hattie in," Gritta said as she tossed another shell into the fire.

Efi stopped scooping the mash from the pot. "'Tis not wise to cast accusations at your neighbors, Gritta. If you are wrong, the sheriff might arrest you."

"At least he would be arresting someone!" Gritta climbed to her feet, aware of the cracking noises emanating from her knees and hips. Age wasn't sneaking up on her; it was overtaking her like a horse and cart. "For all the concern he showed, I would easily believe that Sheriff Werner killed Hattie himself."

"Surely not! The sheriff is a noble-born and far above such behavior."

Gritta rolled her eyes. "Live a few more years, and you might change your opinions of the lordly class."

"He did seem very dismissive of the idea that Hattie was murdered, even after I told him about the marks on her throat," Appel said. "I thought at least he would want to check for himself."

Gritta had been rummaging amongst the empty shells in the basket of hazelnuts, but she stopped and looked at Appel and Efi. "Of all the people in Colmar, Sheriff Werner would have the least trouble removing suspicion from himself. After all, everyone trusts him to catch villains. Who better to become the villain?"

"But why would the sheriff want to kill Hattie Jungerwald? I can think of no reason. Frau Widmer makes much more sense," Efi argued.

"I suppose it could have been Frau Widmer," Appel said slowly, "but I doubt she would be strong enough to strangle someone, even an old woman. And besides, Hattie made a lot of enemies. Just a few days before the murder, I overheard her arguing with Herr Tailleur about the cost of a length of cloth. She claimed he changed the price, and he said she refused to acknowledge their agreement. I've never seen the man so angry."

"And she was wearing a new shift that night, which must have been made of the same cloth. I saw her in it as she stood in the lane," Gritta said. "Herr Tailleur doesn't live far from here, and if he saw her wearing it, it could have enraged him."

"Oh!" Efi cried out, and all three women turned in alarm. Friar Wikerus had approached on the stealthy feet of a man of

God, his plump frame taking up a large part of the doorway and blocking out the light. As usual, a beatific smile lit his face.

"Ah, my dear goodwives, it appears I've interrupted you," he proclaimed, his bright blue eyes twinkling as they took in the bowls of failed brew and reeking piles of scorched barley. All three women stood statue-still, their hearts beating a thunderous chorus in their chests.

"May I come in?" Wikerus stepped inside, and Gritta looked helplessly at Appel. They were done. This meddling man of the church would scold them and then fetch the sheriff or, worse, the prior. Already Gritta could picture the pitiful sight of her younger children begging on the streets while Jorges wandered the countryside, wailing for his lost love. The image of Jorges as a lovelorn wanderer was so funny that Gritta snorted with laughter despite herself, then quickly stifled it. The keen blue gaze landed on her.

"Frau Gritta, I sought you out at your home and was told I could find you here. I came to inquire if your family needs help from the Dominicans, since Jorges cannot work until his arm mends." He was talking to her, but his eyes wandered around the room. "And to admonish you from the temptations of sin, but I see you have already applied yourself to some sort of occupation." He wandered among the vats of mash, peering into them. Efi was still frozen in place, holding her dripping sieve and quaking with fear.

Gritta straightened and thrust out her chin. "As you can see here, Friar Wikerus, we are brewing the season's ale, which God does not prohibit."

"Aye, he does not prohibit it. We also brew our own ale in the priory."

"And if I should allow the good fold of this city to buy my ale to slake their thirst, God would not prohibit that either, for the Proverbist says a good woman makes fine garments and sells them."

"And the word of God also says that wives are to submit to their husbands."

"Even if their husbands are good-for-nothing wastrels?" Gritta shot back. Appel stepped forward, shielding her friend with her tall frame.

"Now, Friar Wikerus, I am sure Gritta would be happy to receive the charity of the Brothers at the priory, but may she also provide for her family by brewing the ale they will drink through the winter? And if she should have a bit of excess, would it not be more industrious of her to sell it to some thirsty traveler instead of waiting for it to go sour so that it is only good for watering the already sodden earth?"

"Wise you are, Frau Appel. God does not approve of waste," Friar Wikerus said, lowering himself onto a bench near the largest pot of mash. "Now, how does this golden water of Dionysus taste?"

The three women glanced uncomfortably at each other. Efi, head hanging, scooped a dipper of ale and handed it to the friar, who sipped tentatively and immediately pulled a face.

"Yech! It's your first attempt, then?"

"Our fifth," Efi said miserably. "Frau Appel's recipe seems to have fled her mind."

"Not fled my mind, you harlot!" Appel erupted before she could catch herself. "'Tis the grain we are using, to be sure. Efi must have sifted it from the straw beneath her cow."

Efi let out a gasp of outrage and prepared to respond, but Wikerus raised both his hands over his head. "Peace, both of you." He sipped from the dipper again.

"Well, of course it's foul to the taste. You've let this malted grain rot in the water for too long. Start over, my dear women, using only a small batch this time. You must get it right before you can make large quantities. Set the malt to rot, but only for as long as it takes to walk from one end of the city to the other. And you must stir it every night and say a prayer over it."

Appel nodded sagely. "Aye. It was the prayin' we did forget."

"And you must use the best water you can find," Wikerus added. "As clear and cool as possible – certainly, you must not use the water in this canal near the tanneries. God cannot help when natural stupidity is driving the cart."

The three women hung their heads but nodded in agreement. For a moment, Wikerus eyed them sternly, then his expression softened. "No, that will not do. Stupid women would sit and wait for their fate to swallow them. You three are more canny than people assume." He hesitated for a moment, and then a slow smile spread on his face. "I'll be back in three days to try your next batch. I expect you will have learned from your mistakes."

True to his word, Friar Wikerus reappeared on the morning of the third day.

"Well." He eased himself onto the bench without being invited. "What have you, then? Anything to show for your labors this week?"

Efi dutifully brought him a dipper of ale once again, and he drank deeply this time, wiping his mouth with his sleeve when he had finished. For a long moment, he was silent.

"Better," he conceded, "but lacking in flavor, other than cloying sweetness. From whom do you purchase your gruit?"

Appel shuffled her feet, edging her way to the door, but Gritta caught her by the sleeve and dragged her back.

"What is gruit?" she hissed. "And why do we need it?"

"'Tis a thing not strictly needed in ale. Kings say so and the city council as well, but they only wish to collect tax from it," Appel muttered.

"Does not the lord God say to give unto Caesar what belongs to Caesar?" Wikerus shot back.

Appel drew herself up. "Now, Friar Wikerus, surely you are not asking a widow to pay more taxes than she can afford? Does not the lord God also say that man is to care for the widowed, the fatherless, and the infirmed?"

"Indeed, wise woman." Wikerus bowed and produced a small, leaf-wrapped parcel from his robe with a flourish. "But you should also consider that the gruit will greatly improve the flavor of your ale. Here is some for you to try. I believe you will find the most success if you mix it with the malt during your boil."

He breezed from the room, and the three women looked at each other helplessly, Appel clutching the little packet of gruit against her chest. Would Wikerus tell the prior? The sheriff? He assured them that he approved of their work, but he was one man out of hundreds in the city. What were they to do?

Gritta pulled in a drag of air and let it out slowly. "Well, my dears, we shall start again, come what may."

"But what is gruit, and how will it help us?" Efi wailed. "For we have wasted so much grain and time. I could have been married and with child by now." She stomped her foot.

"Go then!" Gritta shouted. "Get married! And when your next brainless husband goes off and kills himself in the stupidest way possible, you will be right back where you started!"

"Stop it, both of you!" Appel snapped at the women. "Efi, gruit is a secret mixture of herbs sold by the city council to ensure the ales taste fair and consistent. My dear husband always used it but never told me how he got it nor what was in it." She unwrapped the packet and inspected the contents. "Looks like some rosemary in here and a few sprigs of heather as well."

"You told us that you brewed for your family, Appel." Gritta narrowed her eyes suspiciously.

"Well, I helped." Appel looked at Efi and Gritta, who glared at her, arms crossed over their breasts. "Well, I did not want to let the water ruin my skin, so he did the labor and I consulted on his methods!"

"You said that ale leavings are good for the skin," Efi said coldly.

"I...that is..."

They heard a rush of feet outside the window and then a shout. The three women peered through the open shutters and saw a swelling crowd on the bank of one of the many streams which ran through Les Tanneurs. The throng of people was agitated, yelling and waving their arms.

"Someone fetch the sheriff and the city guard!" a man shouted, and three other men jumped into the shallow water. They heaved together, lifting something heavy and sodden from the murky canal, and the alewives all looked at each other with dread.

"Someone fetch Friar Wikerus," Appel whispered.

In the fray, no one noticed a hooded and robed figure slip from the crowd and disappear into the shadows.

Teeth and knucklebones

In which Friar Wikerus applies to the sheriff for help

F RIAR WIKERUS PULLED HIS rough wool cloak tightly
about his body and shouldered into the cold, damp wind
that blew through the streets of Colmar. On a typical evening,
he would be enjoying a slightly less chilly evening inside his
small cloister in Breisach with his Franciscan brothers, perhaps
engaging in a lively conversation about the divinity of God over
some pottage and a mug of ale before evening prayers. But alas,
since his assignment with the Dominicans for the important
but all-consuming task of identifying the priory's thief, Wikerus
knew there was no time to waste if he wanted to return to his
quiet life.

He staggered through the driving rain to the door of Herr
Schlock's weinstube, where the city's eminent citizens and
councilmen were known to spend their evenings sipping crisp,
pale Alsatian wine and arguing over matters of commerce and
politics. If Friar Wikerus was lucky, Sheriff Werner would be
there as well.

The low-beamed room was warm inside, illuminated only by the light from a large fire in the hearth, which flickered off the faces of the men who sat in small clusters, drinking their wine and eating sausages on brown bread. Friar Wikerus spied Sheriff Werner at a bench in a corner and sat next to him, stretching the toes of his rain-soaked leather boots toward the fire.

"Cold outside, Friar? I thought you would be in prayers right now with the rest of the holy men."

"Normally I would, but the prior has sent me to find you." He leaned closer to the sheriff. "There's been another theft at the church."

The sheriff lowered his cup and put a hand on his forehead. "Saints preserve us! And the theft of the golden cross occurred only weeks ago. I apprehended the thief and have him locked in the cellar of my city house right now." Noticing the patient, flat look on the face of the young friar, the sheriff blushed. "Well now, detaining the man seemed the most sensible thing to do at the time."

"What about this man made him seem like a dishonest knave to you?" Wikerus raised his eyebrows.

"He was a vagrant. Hanging around the Grand Rue, begging for alms. You can never be too careful around a man from Soultz."

"If it was food and shelter he needed, the brothers would have given it to him. I wish you would have told us about this man before you locked him in your cellar, Sheriff Werner." Friar Wikerus tried to keep his voice gentle to hide his frustration. He had joined the order to help the poor and the needy, but they were difficult to save if the local lords got to them first.

"Well, you can have him now if you want because he couldn't have stolen the altar gold if he was in the cellar."

Wikerus sighed heavily and lowered his voice. "It wasn't altar gold stolen this time, Sheriff." He looked left and right to be sure that no one was listening to their conversation. "It was an object from the reliquary."

"What?!" Sheriff Werner leaped to his feet, and the conversations in the room stopped as the men turned to stare at him. Friar Wikerus motioned for the sheriff to seat himself again, which he did uneasily.

"It was the knuckle bone of the fourth finger of Saint Pormin, along with Saint Arbogast's front tooth. A most grave sin because, as you know, this is not just a crime against the prior and the people of Colmar, it is an offense against God."

"Indeed. Whoever committed this atrocity will burn hotly in the fires of hell! May Beelzebub himself and all his demons prod the thief in the arse with their fiery spears!"

"The thief has endangered his mortal soul, and I am sure he's aware of it," Friar Wikerus acknowledged.

"Is there anyone that you suspect, Friar? Anyone inside the priory who might have committed a sin such as this?"

"None of the brothers, of this I am sure."

"Well, Brother Ignatius was supposed to be guarding the altar when the gold cross was taken. What about him? The old fellow always seemed weasel-eyed and shifty to me," Sheriff Werner said, punctuating his declaration with a belch.

"I do not suspect Brother Ignatius, my lord. He is a good and pious man who only wishes to live out the remainder of his days in prayer and contemplation."

"And the laymen? What of the stable hands, the cooks, the washerwomen, and the gardeners?"

Wikerus furrowed his forehead. "The brothers do a good deal of that work themselves, and the few citizens who work at the priory are all trustworthy people who have known Father Konrad for years. Each knows that if he has a need, he can simply ask for help and receive it."

"Well, I think the theft was done by someone inside the order. How else could he find the time to steal when no one else would be in the church? The nave is seldom empty, and the hallways open to the courtyard. It's difficult to sneak about the place."

"Indeed. I shall discuss potential suspected thieves among the brothers with the prior."

There was silence for a moment while each man pondered his wine, then Friar Wikerus spoke again.

"And what of the murder yesterday?"

"Murder? What murder?"

"The woman who was found drowned in the canal in Les Tanneurs. I was nearby when her body was discovered, and a gruesome sight it was."

"Ah." The sheriff waved his comment away. "You must mean Frau Odile, the basket weaver's wife. No, that was not murder, my pious friend. It was an accident of fate. She drowned when she fell in the water."

Friar Wikerus narrowed his eyes. "Truly, it would take some effort to drown in that canal. The water was less than a handspan deep when the workers discovered her body. More now, of course." He looked at the growing puddle of rainwater seeping under the doorway. The walk back to the priory would be a cold one, indeed.

"Perhaps she hit her head first and was knocked senseless. Perhaps she was drunk."

"It has greatly alarmed the population in Les Tanneurs. The three goodwives, Appel, Gritta, and Efi, believe it was the action of a depraved man in our midst." Wikerus leaned closer to the sheriff. "The thief and the murderer could be one and the same person."

The sheriff sighed heavily and wiped a glistening drop of wine from his mustache. "Those three women don't have enough to do. They ought to keep to the business of having children. That will shut off their idle gossip."

"Frau Gritta has twelve children."

"Ah, yes indeed. Well, she mustn't be caring for them properly if she has the time to waste in spreading rumors."

Friar Wikerus pursed his lips. "And the widow, Hattie Jungerwald? Frau Appel Schneider of Les Tanneurs insists that Hattie had marks of strangulation on her throat when she prepared the body for burial."

"Yes, they told me." The sheriff rolled his eyes. "Meddlesome hags. Old women die all the time, but they insist this one was murdered. Well, why not, I ask you! The widow Jungerwald was a scourge on the tradesmen of the city! She owed money everywhere, and it could have been any merchant in town who decided to finish her off."

"But should you not investigate? If her death was not accidental, the killer could strike again."

The sheriff scratched his head. "Well, I do think it might be wise to inquire about the whereabouts of Frau Gritta when Hattie Jungerwald died. If anyone has the temperament for murder, it's that one, har!"

Wikerus stood up and shoved his hands into the sleeves of his robe. "That won't be necessary, Sheriff. I shall talk to Frau Gritta myself. Please come to the priory tomorrow at first light to meet with the prior to discuss the missing relics."

The sheriff smiled drunkenly and elbowed Friar Wikerus a bit too hard in the ribs. "Good lad. What made you so qualified to investigate the theft of church treasures, eh? Did you offend someone in Breisach and have to flee here?"

Friar Wikerus rose quickly to his feet and straightened his belt. "Thank you for your time, my lord. I will let you know what comes of my discussion with Frau Gritta."

And before the sheriff could pull an answer from his wine-stewed brain, Friar Wikerus was out the door, a silhouette rapidly disappearing into the driving rain.

Twelve barrels

In which Jorges reveals an unpleasant side to his character

D ESPITE THE ALEWIVES' INSISTENCE that he need not bother to check in on them, Friar Wikerus reappeared as promised and tasted the new batch of ale, which had the addition of the gruit mixed in. This brew he pronounced "passable" and urged them to feed it to Gritta's family before they decided what to do next. "For you never know," he declared with a satisfied belch, "Gritta's brood may be enough mouths to drain the whole supply with no surplus for selling. No doubt Jorges will guzzle the anything that remains."

"Friar Wikerus, do you not also care for other families in Les Tanneurs? It seems you are here more often than necessary." Appel's voice held an edge of annoyance, but Wikerus did not seem to notice.

"Well, today I am not here to taste this fine ale you've produced. I also wanted to inquire about your church habits. I have only seen Frau Appel in the church this week and none of you last Lord's Day. Are you attending in a different city, or do you avoid the church to escape the confession and forgiveness of your sins?" He looked straight at Gritta.

"I've been busy. With Jorges lamed, there is twice the work and none of the thanks for it. Not any money, neither."

Friar Wikerus nodded. "You must be in dire need of coin, Frau Gritta. How do you manage to feed your children with no able-bodied man to earn your bread?"

"I've got some coppers hid in a safe place." Gritta sniffed. "We ain't as poor as the people say."

"But you told the sheriff only a few weeks ago that you hadn't any money to release Jorges from the pillory. How is it that you came by enough to feed so many children in such a short time?"

Gritta narrowed her eyes. "Do you suspect me of stealing the money or selling myself? I had that money put by when the sheriff came over, but I didn't use it to free Jorges from the pillory because I need to fill the bellies of my children." She looked around the room. Appel and Efi looked back solemnly. "There, you see, girls? I am making a confession to this holy man right now. I did lie to the lord sheriff and allow my husband to stay in captivity longer than necessary."

"Your sins are forgiven," Friar Wikerus said absently, "but where did that money come from, Gritta?"

Appel stepped forward and put a protective hand on her friend's shoulder. "Thank you for coming to see we're doing this proper, Friar. Now, I am sure you must have important work amongst the poor and invalid in the city." She took his arm and led him to the door.

"Yes, yes." Wikerus nodded, his cheeks rosy from the ale. "It is time I was off. Oh, and Frau Appel—" he turned and stopped on his way out the door "— I am pleased, for you followed my advice about using cleaner water. Am I to understand that this water comes from Herr Gerhard's portion of the canal? Truly excellent. I can taste its purity. I shall thank him for allowing you to use it."

"No need, Friar Wikerus," Appel muttered under her breath.

With a cheerful goodbye, Friar Wikerus was off, and Efi slammed the door behind him.

"Oh!" Efi wailed. "What shall we do? He is sure to betray us."

"There's no law against us brewing," Appel said firmly. "Not one that's written on vellum, anyhow. Better we brew than become castle washerwomen." She meant to spit on the ground to punctuate her disapproval but caught a sharp glance from Gritta. Gritta's oldest daughter, Lisette, was a castle washerwoman and a well-known favorite of Lord Frider, whose modest fortress stuck up like a stone pimple on the gently rolling hills outside the city walls.

"Anyhow," Gritta said coolly, "one thing is sure, we should not try to sell this ale ourselves. There are too many of this village who would take offense, even if Appel did convince Herr Gerhard to give us better water. How did you manage that, Appel?"

Appel muttered something about a long-standing agreement with Herr Gerhard that no one could quite hear and then stood to pour herself a cup of ale.

"Anyway," Gritta continued, "Appel is right. We need a hood."

"A what?"

"A hood. You know, someone to be the cover over our faces. A shield between the villagers and us."

For a moment, they were silent. Appel and Gritta had lived in the community all their lives. They knew everyone in this city, but there was not one person among their lifelong neighbors that they trusted to front their brewing operation. Efi was useless, as usual, because of her newness to the area. She cleared her throat and ventured her own comment.

"It would be helpful if our hood were a man, would it not? A man wouldn't be troubled by the law as we would..." She looked straight at Gritta.

Appel sighed when she understood Efi's unspoken meaning. "Indeed. If only there were a man around who seemed to have the time on his hands to sell and knew the taste of a good ale."

"One who the other men knew was a true drinker of the stuff," Efi said helpfully. "A connoisseur."

"Oh, stop it, both of you!" Gritta yelled. "Jorges is not fit to walk in a straight line or to sell ale, no less. He will drink all of it before it is in the hands of honest folk, mark me. That is why we chose to brew here and not at my cottage."

"That is why he is a perfect hood for us. No one would be surprised at the sight of Jorges selling the drink as well as consuming it. And this ale isn't terribly strong – not like wine. Here you can satisfy his need to drink without wasting all your earnings," Efi implored, and Gritta nodded reluctantly. There was sense in this scheme, although she hated to acknowledge when Efi was right. Conceding that Jorges was useful for something was equally difficult to admit.

And so they agreed that Jorges would sell the ale, which would be unsurprising to the the residents of Les Tanneurs, who were used to seeing his inebriated form staggering through the streets of Colmar. It was also very suspect, since Jorges was assured to be even more consistently intoxicated than usual. Several village women came to visit Gritta, baskets looped into the crooks of their elbows, their wimples arranged around their temples and shoulders. Are you sure, they asked, that it is a good idea for Jorges to brew? Would it not bring troubles upon the neighborhood? Gritta reassured them that Jorges was a competent salesman, and she silently promised God that she would confess her lies to a priest in church come the Lord's Day.

For his part, Jorges was delighted to feel important. He accepted the invitation from his wife with a nod of his head and a lengthy speech about how his superior instinct for commerce would do them all good. Then he swaggered about the city, ducking into the inn so he could sample the ale and then spit it out violently, proclaiming it to be spoiled.

"A pity you sell this swill, Karl," he said to the innkeeper one day, so all could hear. "My ale is not only finer tasting but also cheaper since it doesn't come all the way from Strassburg or Vogelgrun. Why, for the cost and time it takes you to get your ale from another city, I could sell you twice as much!"

This caught Karl's attention, and by the end of the day, Jorges swayed home singing loudly after an afternoon of celebrating his first sale. He tripped over the threshold of Appel's door and stumbled into the house, where the women were taking their ease after boiling a new mash.

"Here you all are, laying about like Lady Marguerite on her couch while I'm a'working down at the inn, selling more ale than you three could possibly brew."

"Jorges, you're drunk. Tomorrow's your day to unload the ships at the docks now that your arm is mended." Gritta rolled her eyes. "He will never wake in time," she said to the others.

"Quiet, woman!" Jorges wobbled across the room and sat heavily on a bench. "You treat me like a fool. Well, would a fool sell twelve barrels of ale to Karl the innkeeper, due for delivery tomorrow, eh?"

Appel drew herself up. "You are a fool, Jorges Leporteur! Twelve barrels you sold to Karl Gastwirt?! How will we ever brew enough to satisfy an order so large? We don't even possess twelve sound barrels to store so much ale."

"Don't it take just a day to make twelve barrels?" Jorges hiccoughed. Appel stepped closer.

"No, and neither can we find enough grain for the mash, nor can we afford enough gruit! Only a dullard would make promises that are impossible to keep. If we cannot fill such an order to the only reputable inn in the city, how will other customers ever trust us? You have made a stupid mistake, you sot!"

Jorges steadied himself against the wall. "Wife!" He declared haughtily to Gritta, "Come! I forbid you to spend time with these idle whores. Get home and take care of the children."

"The children are all asleep, Jorges," Gritta said weakly. "I saw to them before I came to Appel's house."

Jorges strode across the room with surprising speed and slapped Gritta hard across the face. "Do not defy me, woman! I am your husband, your master, and you had best do as I say!"

"That is enough!" Appel roared, jumping to her feet and brandishing her wooden mash paddle like a spear.

Jorges took his wife's hand and pulled her roughly from the house into the darkness. The sound of Jorges slamming the door behind him echoed through the dark, quiet lane as Efi and Appel looked at each other helplessly.

The Lord's bounty

In which the alewives don't let bruises stop them

G RITTA DID NOT LEAVE her house for three days. Appel watched her friend's door from across the lane, hands on her hips and apprehension clouding her face, every day until she could stand it no longer. Putting on her best bonnet and hooking her arm on a basket of good pears from her larder, she marched across Trench Lane to Gritta's cottage. Without bothering to knock, she pushed her way inside.

Jorges was snoring on a pile of straw near the partition that kept the animals in the winter, with his legs and arms splayed. Gritta sat beside the fire, listlessly stirring a pot that hung suspended on an iron hook over the coals. Her two youngest children, Wina and Egilhard, tugged on her skirts, alternately crying and hitting her legs with their chubby fists. The room was dark, damp, and too warm.

"There now," Appel cooed, hoisting little Wina to her hip. "Come, children, let's help your ma prepare the afternoon meal." She set Egilhard to work wiping the table and gave Wina a juicy pear before sending her outside to play. Then she gently approached her friend.

Gritta continued to face the fire, saying nothing.

"Come, Frau Gritta, you're not the kind of woman who takes her ease in front of the hearth like some idle cat," Appel said with a frown. Gritta stopped stirring and turned to her. Appel covered her mouth in shock. The right half of Gritta's face was puffy and covered in purple bruises.

"It's not the first time Jorges has struck me," Gritta said, looking back at the flames, "but it's the worst. He doesn't like being challenged, Appel. You should not have said those things to him."

"Then he ought to have come to my house and tried to hit me in the face! That good-for-nothing winesop would get more in return than he gave out!"

"Did you deliver the twelve barrels of ale?" Gritta asked.

"No. Jorges came to the house and took everything we had to Karl, but it was only three barrels. Karl seems pleased, however. Did Jorges hand over the coin?"

Gritta shook her head sadly. "Never saw any coin. Not so much as a copper or a cockerel for the porridge pot. It was a bad idea to use Jorges as our hood. He is no longer the man I married. He's a lout and a scoundrel."

Appel sat heavily near Gritta. "It was not your decision. I suggested it, and we all went along with my plan."

A shadow darkened the doorway and the two women looked up. Efi stood on the threshold, holding Wina's hand.

"I found this little beauty covered in ants and sticky pear," she laughed. "Oh, my dear Gritta," Efi gasped when she saw the bruising. "Will cabbage leaves help?"

Despite themselves, Gritta and Appel threw their heads back and laughed. "You aren't terribly bright, Efi, but you're a welcome sight all the same," Appel said. "Run across the lane to my garden and fetch the last of my comfrey. There's still a bit left. We'll make a poultice for Gritta's face, and then—"

She stopped short. Another shadow darkened the doorway. This time it was Karl Gastwirt, the innkeeper, along with Herr Adolphe, the barber-surgeon. The two men greeted Gritta heartily, although Adolphe grew concerned when he saw the bruises on her face. "Will you be needing my services, Frau Gritta?" he asked.

"No indeed, for Efi is fetching a poultice for me." Gritta winced as she spoke. In the corner, little Egilhard watched the men with wide eyes, still clutching the cloth he used to wipe the table.

"We've come for Jorges," Karl said. "Is he here?"

"No, Jorges is off for Vogelgrun to lift crates at the docks today," Gritta answered with a pained curtsey. "'Tis his regular work, and only on the ides of the month does he work in Lord Frider's fields."

Karl frowned. "A pity. I came to get some more of that fine ale from him."

"And I as well, for I need it for my patients," Adolphe put in. "It's a strange-tasting brew but powerfully fit for healing, I can tell you that. I used to buy my ale from Hattie Jungerwald, but since she passed, I've been trying to make it myself. Tastes like hog slop."

Appel and Efi both looked at Gritta, who stood on stiff legs. "Well, Jorges is not here, but I am most willing to take your order."

Karl ignored her and looked around the main room of the house, taking in the flaking plaster that showed the willow thatch underneath, the dirt floor, and the crumbling hearth.

"Don't see no cauldrons for brewing. Where does Jorges do it, Frau Gritta? How does he create such a flavorful brew? It tastes good but doesn't intoxicate my customers, so they spend more coin to get just as drunk as they normally would."

"Where does Jorges brew…" Gritta trailed off. Was Jorges telling people that he made this ale by himself? Gritta leaped to her feet, despite her pain. "The unholy nerve of that man!"

"He told me he called this ale forth by the power of his pure talent. I never knew he had a talent for brewing, Frau Gritta, only drinking."

"Oh, he has a talent, alright, Herr innkeeper. Just when I think he has rightly chastised me, his slow wits reminds me who has the upper hand."

Karl and Adolphe looked at each other, helpless in the face of Gritta's fury. Karl bowed slightly.

"Well, when he returns, will you please tell him that my guests have been asking about that golden ale he sold us? Excellent stuff, it is, and they'll pay for it. I couldn't keep it very long because they drank me dry. He only delivered three, but I will still put in for twelve barrels if I can."

The men departed, and the three women stared after them, dumbstruck.

"I think we may have a talent for this," Efi said tentatively.

"A talent indeed! Girls, tie up your skirts. We're going to go back to my house to brew!" Appel leapt to her feet.

"But, Appel dear, we haven't enough grain for so much ale—and the time besides. How will my Noe ever make twelve barrels?"

Efi's eyes danced. "Can I tell her please, Frau Appel?"

"Tell me what?" Gritta asked.

With an excited squeal, Efi had Gritta by the arm and dragged her across Trench Lane to Appel's house. Gritta couldn't believe her eyes. There near the hearth were four massive pots bubbling with fermenting mash.

"It is a miracle, Frau Gritta!" Efi squealed. "When Appel woke one morning to use the privy, she discovered pots and bags of grain waiting outside her door!"

Gritta turned to Appel, who nodded her head, grinning.

"I did my business in the privy right quick that morning, I'll tell you. We must have a patron or a guardian angel."

"Is this enough to fill Karl's order?"

"Yes, it should be."

"But who sent it?" Efi asked.

"Who, indeed?" Gritta gave Appel a sideways look and noticed that her friend blushed and turned aside.

"Come," Appel said, pushing her sleeves up to her elbows. "Let us go to work straightaway and take payment from Karl before Jorges returns from Vogelgrun!"

Efi began to stoke the fire, and Appel measured grain for malting while Gritta trotted across Trench Lane to find some of her children to bring the water from Herr Gerhard's stream. Soon, the large house was humming with chatter and laughter and the faint popping of barley as it toasted gently over the low coals. The women and children worked merrily all morning, singing and telling stories while the house filled with the damp, musty heat of fermenting mash and herbs.

Gritta's son Noe, who was apprenticed to the cooper, arrived with two more barrels for the ale. They were ugly but sound and watertight, despite their appearance, and Gritta glowed with pride. He may not make a handsome barrel, but one of her children might just amount to something.

After they set the morning's brew aside to ferment, they borrowed a two-wheeled cart, and together the three women dragged the barrels into the heart of the city to deliver to the inn, followed by a crowd of delighted children who shouted and threw pebbles at them.

"Here now!" Gritta roared ferociously, using her best scolding voice. "One more o' you little chits throws a rock at me and you shall see my slipper warm your arse!"

"Be still, Gritta, and pull your weight," Appel groaned. "See, we are nearly there."

When the barrels were unloaded and Gritta's palm full of coins, they dragged the cart back and retreated to Appel's house to divide their spoils. That night, Gritta treated her children to a hindquarter of pork with stewed plums, and they all went to sleep, their stomachs gurgling pleasantly with the unexpected bounty.

From then on, the golden brew made by the alewives of Colmar was in high demand. Jorges eventually slunk back to the house from his week at the docks as a porter and made overtures of apology to his wife, whose bruises were still visible on her jaw. He sold three more barrels of ale to Adolphe, the barber-surgeon, and he insisted on making the delivery himself, which also meant taking the payment on their behalf. When he returned, he presented each woman with three copper coins.

The work and materials involved in brewing the ale warranted more than three copper coins, and the women knew that Jorges held back a considerable sum for himself. They could hear the money jingling in his scrip.

"Gritta, my dear neighbor, I love you, but your husband is a louse-ridden nuisance, and make no mistake about that," Appel commented one afternoon.

"We should kill him," Efi snarled, and the other two women stopped their work to stare at her for a moment.

"Well, everyone else is killing off those they do not want around, so why not us?"

And in that moment, they became aware that they were not alone. There was a quick knock at the door, and it swung open. Frau Widmer, Hattie Jungerwald's quarrelsome neighbor, poked her head inside.

"Ho, Appel! I've come for the peck of wheat flour that you owe me."

Appel sighed. Now that Hattie Jungerwald was dead and Frau Widmer was without her sworn enemy to keep her occupied during the waning days of summer, she had been making more of a nuisance of herself to the other goodwives of Les Tanneurs.

"I repaid you the wheat flour yesterday, Frau Widmer, with this sack, see?" Appel held up a hemp sack that spat a little puff of white powder.

"Ah, but there was some room in my cup when you returned it, and I want it all back. I'm preparing to take some honey cakes to Herr Hansel's oven today. I wish to celebrate my good fortune." She waved a small clay cup in the air.

"What good fortune do you have, Frau Widmer?" Efi asked as she measured barley into her basket. "Surely it is an extravagance to spend your oven money on cakes instead of your daily bread."

"Let us hope someone offered to move you to another city. That would be good fortune for all of us," Gritta mumbled.

"That is none of your business, young Efi," Frau Widmer snapped. "Come, Appel, pay what you owe." She thrust the cup under Appel's nose. "Fill it to the top, if you please."

"Frau Widmer," Appel said as she took the cup and opened her sack. "I give this flour to you not because I think you are right but because I wish to avoid a confrontation with you in front of these children." She motioned to Gritta's children, Wina, Anstett, and Mattheus, who all watched with vicious anticipation. "I understand why Hattie Jungerwald called you a she-scoundrel."

"How dare you!" Frau Widmer shrieked.

Appel handed her the cup of flour and stabbed a finger at her door. "Out, now."

"I wouldn't stay in this house for one more minute if you gave me your entire flour sack. You are a witch and a putrelle, Appel!" Frau Widmer shouted and whirled to leave. As she did, the skirts of her dress flounced, and Gritta caught sight of a white linen chemise with dark brown embroidery along the hem. As soon as the door slammed, she turned to the other women.

"It was her!" Gritta hissed. "Frau Widmer is wearing Hattie Jungerwald's new chemise – the one that was removed from her body after she died! When Hattie was shouting in the street on the night of her murder, she was clad only in that chemise."

"Are you sure?"

"Aye, for it has dark stitching along the hem in the pattern of leaves and flowers."

"And Frau Widmer did accuse Hattie of being a thief during their argument," Efi said slowly. "So, she must have stolen the shift back again after Hattie was dead."

Gritta slapped her hand on her thigh. "Appel! What was Hattie wearing when you went to prepare the body?"

"A chemise, but it wasn't white with dark stitching; it was white with red stitching. That garment was removed from Hattie's body at some point either right before or immediately after her death."

"Yes, it makes sense! Frau Widmer killed Hattie Jungerwald, then changed her into an old chemise and took the new one!"

"But," Efi interjected, "why would you kill someone for a piece of underclothing? Embroidered or not, it seems a risk to take for a piece of clothing that is not difficult to make."

"Frau Widmer is motivated by greed and pettiness. I wouldn't put it past her to kill someone for a piece of underclothing." Gritta crossed her arms over her breasts. "And how do we know there wasn't some more compelling reason? After all, she and Hattie have been feuding for years."

"Well, we must confront her, but how can we do it? If she really killed Hattie, she could do it again."

"Let us call for the sheriff and discuss it with him. He will bear witness and protect us."

"And he also told us outright that he doesn't care if poor women are murdered in his city, and I am not about to become the next corpse that he buries without a second thought," Appel snapped.

For a moment they were all quiet.

"We must trick her into a confession," said Gritta. "And make sure the sheriff is present when it happens."

"That sounds impossible. Frau Widmer would never confess to anything, and the sheriff will not do as we ask."

"We could tie him up," Efi suggested and then cringed when she saw the shocked expressions on the faces of the two older women. "And we could tie her up too! Make her confess under threat of harm."

"Are you suggesting we torture Frau Widmer, Efi?" Appel said, stunned. "I dislike the woman, but I dislike the threat of hell even more."

"No," Gritta said firmly. "It must be a willing confession, and the sheriff doesn't need to be present. We shall invite her to taste the ale and then see what comes."

Sloth and drunkenness

In which Frau Widmer provides her expertise

L IKE MANY OF THE goodwives of the city, Frau Widmer brewed her own ale for use in her household. She was all too delighted to come and "provide counsel" when Appel invited her to try the alewives' brew. She scooped a dipper into the cauldron with a bony hand and sipped, her sparse eyelashes fluttering as she pondered the taste.

"'Tis too strong. You will make your children drunk on this ale," she declared.

"Indeed." Gritta stepped forward and offered her another dipper. "This is not for the children but for the men when they require a strong drink to help them forget their troubles."

Frau Widmer sipped again. "Does the prior know that you are brewing strong ale? He disapproves of sloth and drunkenness."

"We will inform the prior in good time," Appel cooed. "Take another drink, Frau Widmer, and tell us your thoughts on the flavor of the herbs. Did I add too much bog myrtle?"

Frau Widmer sipped again, rolling the brew across her tongue like the proprietor of a weinstube. "The flavor is...interesting.

Doesn't taste like most strong ales. You must have used too much rosemary."

"Try again," Efi encouraged her. "Can you taste anything else in this brew that you recognize?"

By now, Frau Widmer's cheeks were growing rosy, and she smiled at Efi, patting her face with a sun-withered hand. "Such a sweet, pretty girl you are, Efi! It won't be long before you find another husband with those golden curls and that plump figure."

Appel and Gritta exchanged a knowing look, and Efi urged Frau Widmer onto a bench, discreetly plucking the hem of the woman's skirt to reveal the white chemise underneath with the dark brown stitching.

"Why Frau Widmer, this chemise is positively beautiful! Where did you get such a fine thing?"

For a moment, Frau Widmer's eyes narrowed, and she lowered her cup.

"Don't you even think of taking it from me. It was already stolen once from my drying line. I haven't taken it off since I got it back from the thievin' whore who stole it from me." She leaned into Gritta's shoulder and whispered loudly, "I've been a'wearing it since the feast of Saint Pancras."

Gritta wrinkled her nose and looked at Appel, for everyone knew that not washing one's laundry was one of the basest forms of ill hygiene. Frau Widmer swayed and held her cup up to Efi, who quickly refilled it. "I got my revenge," she declared.

"No one will steal laundry from my line after what I did to that old hag!"

Now all three alewives all edged closer. Efi batted her eyelashes in false innocence. "Whatever do you mean, Frau Widmer? How does one teach a lesson to a laundry thief?"

Frau Widmer belched and leaned her back against the wall. "Never you mind, Efi dear. It's clear that God was on my side, and my laundry won't go walking away on another woman's shoulders again."

Gritta was about to put another question to her now very drunk neighbor when the door opened, and Jorges burst in, singing loudly and tripping over the cat. Frau Widmer's lopsided smile turned downwards and she stood.

"Well, I had best be going now. See that you follow my advice and weaken your ale, or I will be forced to tell the prior of your sinful brew. God is displeased when his flock holds secrets."

After Frau Widmer flounced unsteadily from the house, the three women looked at each other.

"It was her," Efi hissed. Not only is she wearing the same chemise that Gritta saw on Hattie Jungerwald, but she practically admitted to committing the crime herself!"

Appel's forehead wrinkled. "So what about this sudden fortune she claims to have? Where would she have gotten money unless someone in Colmar gave it to her? Did she kill Hattie from pure spite, or was there a profit in it?"

"Or from Odile. After all, Frau Widmer didn't get on well with Odile either, and the poor woman was drowned in the canal."

"The sheriff believes that drowning was an accident," Efi said.

"Weren't no accident," a male voice surprised them. They had forgotten that Jorges was also in the room. "I was there when they pulled Frau Odile's body from the canal. No one could drown in that water unless someone held them down. The canal was not even deep enough to cover your ankles."

Appel stood and began to pace, one hand on her chin. "What do Hattie Jungerwald and Frau Odile have in common?"

"They are both from Les Tanneurs," Efi volunteered.

"They were both enemies of Frau Widmer," Appel mused.

"And they were both dismissed as accidents by Sheriff Werner," Gritta said grimly. "I've said it before, and I'll say it again; the man is in the best position to hide a murder."

"But why? What could be his motivation for killing two poor women in Les Tanneurs and then covering up the deaths?"

"Perhaps he didn't kill them himself." Now Gritta was on her feet as well, pacing next to Appel. "Perhaps he is protecting the person who did kill them."

"But who could the sheriff possibly want to protect?" Appel asked. "His kin all died in the pestilence. Who else could there be?"

Altar gold

In which a trap remains unsprung

B ROTHER WIKERUS STARED AT the altar in shock and disappointment. Standing tall on the table, gleaming dully in the flickering light, were two gold candlesticks covered in dripping wax. He turned to the short young friar who sat dejectedly on the altar steps.

"And you never left your post? Not once?"

The friar shook his head mournfully. "Not once, Brother Wikerus. Not even to the courtyard wall to go for a piss."

Wikerus stroked his chin and began to pace.

"Perhaps the thief knew you were here? Perhaps he saw you hiding and did not come near for fear of being caught. I have told no one else of this plan, so there is no way he could have known we had set a trap for him."

"I did as you said and hid myself directly beneath the altar cloth; God forgive me." The little friar crossed himself quickly. "I saw men enter and leave the chapel for prayers, but as you can see, nothing was stolen. The rats even left the bread alone today."

"Did you see the faces of those that entered?" Brother Wikerus asked sharply.

"Aye, indeed. Father Konrad, followed by the brothers, and Frau Henninga, who came to wash the floors."

Brother Wikerus looked up. "Who?"

"Frau Henninga. She occasionally asks to wash the floors of the church with her hair as a way to flagellate herself in penance before God, like Mary Magdalene when she washed and dried the feet of Christ with her own hair."

"How curious," Brother Wikerus mused, a memory tugging at him.

"She's been washing the floors since before the prior's appointment here. He didn't feel it fit to stop her."

"And Frau Henninga also in the church when the gold cross was stolen, was she not?"

"Aye, she came to do some sweeping up that night."

"Interesting." Friar Wikerus scratched his chin.

There was a scraping sound as the door in the narthex was dragged open, and two figures entered. The widows Appel and Efi walked forward quietly, wearing their best dresses, heads covered with crisp white wimples, and genuflected when they entered the nave. Appel looked up, surprised to see that they were not alone.

"Greetings, Friar Wikerus. Efi and I have just come to request prayers of mercy for our departed husbands that they may avoid the fires of hell and damnation."

Beside her, Efi sniffled and wiped her eyes with a linen handkerchief. Friar Wikerus smiled.

"You are good to think of the departed. Shall I call one of the brothers inside to intercede on your behalf?"

He nodded to the young friar, who hurried off into the darkness. Then, with a great sigh, Wikerus began removing the candlesticks from the altar while Efi looked on curiously.

"Why do you remove those candlesticks, Friar? Should you not keep them here?"

"As you may have heard," Friar Wikerus said, tucking one of the gold altarpieces into an iron-banded trunk. "We have a thief who has been stealing gold from the church. It is necessary that we keep the altar gold under iron until we determine who the thief is and have him placed on trial for defiling God's house."

Appel clucked her tongue and shook her head. "A grave sin, indeed. What kind of a fiend would steal from God himself? Only one who is the most familiar with God and his ways, and the most confident in his ability to gain absolution, no doubt."

Efi looked at Appel, her brow knit. "Appel, do you accuse one of the Dominican brothers?"

"Who else would have such free access to the altar?"

Friar Wikerus placed an iron lock on the box and turned the key, which hung from a leather strap affixed to his belt.

"No, dear alewives, I do not think one of our own took the altar gold. The fear of God is greater for them. Only one who is not fully acquainted with the power of God's wrath would endanger himself in such a way."

The young friar returned to the knave with a thin, scowling Dominican following him.

"Father Tacitus is here to intercede for you goodwives as you pray for the souls of your departed husbands."

Father Tacitus nodded sourly to the two women and stepped upon the dais of the altar. He began to intone in Latin.

"Requiem æternam dona ei, Domine. Et lux perpetua luceat ei. Requiescat in pace. Amen."

Everyone crossed themselves, and the sour-faced Dominican stepped down from the altar and placed a hand upon Efi's wimple-covered head as she knelt, saying a lengthy prayer and then repeating the process with Appel.

"Don't know why you couldn't have done that yourself, Friar Wikerus," Father Tacitus snarled under his breath as he turned to walk from the room. Friar Wikerus sighed. He was on good-enough terms with most of the holy men of the priory, but Father Tacitus had a determinedly bitter attitude.

"Frau Appel, do you know where to find the house of Frau Henninga?" he asked.

"Indeed, she lives with her son's family outside the walls, just yonder." Appel pointed to the north, and Friar Wikerus thanked her. The young friar next to him tugged on his sleeve.

"Do you believe that Frau Henninga is the one who has been stealing the gold, Brother Wikerus?"

Efi covered her mouth in shock, and even Appel looked affronted. Friar Wikerus shot an annoyed glance at the friar, who cringed next to him, instantly realizing his mistake.

"Surely you do not accuse Frau Henninga of stealing the altar gold, Friar? Why, she has been a loyal servant of this church all her life. She only didn't join the nuns herself because she lacked the funds for a proper donation after her husband died."

"Well, if she is the thief, she would certainly have the funds for a donation now!" Brother Adolph chirped.

"I only wish to talk to her, that is all. The altar gold has gone missing several times while she has been at the priory to wash the floors."

Appel crossed her arms. "And yet it didn't go missing today." She nodded to the locked box.

"Indeed, but that is because I had Brother Adolph here, hiding to keep watch. No one could have taken the gold without him witnessing the deed."

"And she saw him hiding, then?" Appel asked defensively.

"She was washing the floors, so she could have spied his feet from where he hid under the altar."

Appel drew herself up. "Friar! I am surprised that I, a humble goodwife and widow of a faithful man, must be the one to chastise you for hiding a young and impressionable friar underneath God's sacred altar!"

Despite himself, Friar Wikerus felt his face glowing with embarrassment. All of this was out of control.

"Only because it was a dire circumstance, Frau Appel. Only because I meant to protect God's priceless objects."

"Aye! The thief even stole off with Saint Pormin's knucklebone!" the young friar said breathlessly, and Friar Wikerus turned to him in exasperation.

"Do you not have some prayers to say, Brother Adolph?"

The young man hung his head, crossed himself at the altar, shoved his hands into the sleeves of his robe, and shuffled from the room, his feet scraping loudly against the stone, which, Friar Wikerus noted, was still damp from Frau Henninga's cleaning. He turned to the two widows, noting their distrustful expressions.

"Please excuse me, for I must pay a visit to Frau Henninga. Perhaps she didn't take the gold, but she might have information about who was coming and going in the nave while she worked. Determining the identity of the thief is a task best suited for a man anyhow. The two of you should return to your own homes before nightfall."

He walked quickly from the church and out into the rapidly encroaching twilight.

The accused

In which the alewives realize they have solved the mystery

E FI WAS INSIDE GRITTA'S house, helping with the wool-dying when she heard the shrill whine of Frau Widmer's voice outside.

"Where is she? Let me at the thieving wench. I'll tear her limbs off!"

The door slammed open, and there stood Frau Widmer in all her scrawny furor, strands of mousy-brown hair flying from underneath her brown linen cap. She thrust an accusatory finger at Gritta.

"And just where did you get that wool, Frau Gritta?" Frau Widmer screeched. "My sack of white wool, which I had kept in my larder, is gone, and I know you had seen it because you asked me where I had purchased it last spring. Well, I told Girard, the night watchman, to be extra careful around my house. He's on the lookout for you!"

"Indeed, and after I spied your sack of fine white wool, I went and purchased my own from the same shepherd," Gritta said calmly. "Why would I steal anything from you?"

Frau Widmer leaned in close. "Because you're poor and overburdened with children, that's why. You know I have wealth, and you want to take it from me. Just like that thieving Hattie did! Well, she got what was coming to her. Both of them did!"

Efi and Gritta looked at each other for a moment. "Both of them, Frau Widmer?"

"Odile Lepanier took my best crock – right from my larder. And look what happened. She turned up dead in a ditch. God is clearly on my side, Gritta. You and any other wench who tries to steal from me had best be careful of his retribution. The righteous finger of God smites all who oppose me!"

Gritta rose to her feet. "Frau Widmer, I can think of no reason why Odile would walk into your larder and steal a crock when I know perfectly well that she had a superior one in her own home. And if you come near me with intent to harm, I'll tell everyone that you let pocky old Jacques Mendiant tup you in a turnip field the day before you wed your long-suffering husband!"

Frau Widmer's eyes widened until they looked ready to pop from her head. She spun and slammed the door on her way out, leaving Efi and Gritta stunned. Efi turned to Gritta.

"Is that true?"

Gritta shrugged. "Probably. She certainly seemed to think it true. There were always rumors about her and Jacques Mendiant."

"All of those threats she keeps making...it really makes her seem so guilty of Hattie and Odile's murders. I know you suspect the sheriff, but I still see no reason for him to want those women dead." Efi grunted as she agitated the barrel of wet wool with a stick.

"If only we hadn't been interrupted while we were questioning her," Gritta said, clenching her teeth. "One more dipper of our strong wormwood ale, and we would have had the whole story from her, of that I am sure."

"She was so close, but now we'll never get her to talk to us candidly again."

"I'm not sure we need to," Gritta said, plunging her hands into the tub massaging the dye into the wool. "She is certainly not being very careful. Why, she practically admitted to plotting my murder right here on my doorstep."

Efi hefted the wet mat of fiber from the water with her stick, wrung the wool out, and inspected it. She had been the one to add the weld-flowers to the dye concoction. Instead of a buttery-yellow, the wool was the same vibrant orange of a sunflower. "Oh, is this too much?"

Gritta inspected the work.

"No, it is perfect. That color will flatter little Wina and Rosmunda as well. I aim to make this yarn into shawls for the both of them."

The two women worked for the rest of the day, telling jokes and chatting with neighbors who stopped by the house to visit. Jorges was working at the docks and had been away for two days, so when the innkeeper's hired boy came by to collect a barrel of ale, Gritta and Efi washed their hands, changed their wimples, and escorted him to Appel's house across Trench Lane.

Appel was inside at her bench near the window, knitting and humming to herself. When Efi and Gritta apprised her of their visit from Frau Widmer, Appel furrowed her brow and paced the room a few times.

"But it's too obvious, isn't it? I saw Hattie purchase that very same white linen from the cloth seller myself, and Gritta, you saw her wearing the finished product of her labors. Why would she steal laundry from Frau Widmer? And you're right; Odile had her own crock. I know because I helped her prepare the season's cabbage on several occasions at her house and packed it into that very crock myself."

"It's almost as if Frau Widmer is trying to make herself look guilty," Efi added.

Gritta crossed her arms and huffed. "You both are forgetting something: Frau Widmer is paranoid and dim-witted. I, for one, think that she is making idle threats. It's a coincidence that Hattie and Odile were murdered."

"That is an awfully strong coincidence, Gritta. You were the one who suspected Widmer in the first place."

"But that is before I remembered that she wastes so much energy being suspicious of her neighbors that she couldn't possibly have any strength left to kill with her bare hands."

On the other side of the room, the innkeeper's assistant lifted one of the tuns of ale and staggered under its weight to his two-wheeled cart. Appel's eyes strayed to him and lingered for a moment on the muscles of his back as he strained to pick up another tun. Gritta cleared her throat pointedly, and Appel's eyes darted back.

"Very well, but can we all agree that the woman is at odds with every other goodwife in Les Tanneurs? The only women she hasn't accused of wronging her are those who can afford to live in the better parts of Colmar."

Appel and Efi nodded their heads.

"What did she mean when she said she had come into some money? She's the wife of a tanner, too. Her husband may have a good clientele and be a guild member, but he's not wealthy," Gritta said.

"And she's not selling wares in the market," Appel mused. "She minds the house and her children."

"Perhaps she is brewing and selling her ale, like us! She stole our idea!" Efi cried out.

"Efi, don't you start. We're not all constantly stealing from each other," Gritta laughed.

"She could have come into money if she had something valuable to sell...such as altar gold."

"You aren't suggesting that Frau Widmer has the intelligence to evade the sheriff and Friar Wikerus while also murdering her neighbors, do you?" Gritta asked.

"It makes sense. How else could she acquire money?" Efi crossed her arms. "And maybe she's only evading Friar Wikerus. Perhaps she is the one that the sheriff is protecting."

"But why?" Appel threw her hands up in the air. "There is no reason for it!"

"I do not think she is stealing the gold, but she could have sold her crock and then claimed Odile stole it."

"Well," Appel sighed, "I suppose we ought to find the sheriff and tell him. It would solve two murders, and even he can't ignore that many deaths in his city."

"But if we suspect the sheriff, we shouldn't tell him, Appel."

"You're right, of course. The prior, then. I've known Father Konrad all my life, and he knows me. I will approach him with the matter." Appel dusted her hands against each other and stood up.

They opened the door and looked out into the darkness of the night, where a chilly autumn rain blew in sideways sheets.

Gritta turned to Appel. "Tomorrow?"

"Aye, tomorrow. Keep your door barred tonight, Gritta. If she is the murderer, I would say that she has you targeted for her next strike."

"I'll do more than keep my door barred," Gritta muttered.

The next day was Saint Nestor's day, and the women knew they could find Father Konrad in the church. After the end of the service, in which the prior admonished the congregation in fiery Latin, Appel, Efi, and Gritta, who carried Wina on one arm and dragged Egilhard with the other, all rushed at the man of God as he retreated from the nave. Upon seeing the three alewives of Les Tanneurs, the prior felt an urgent need to quicken his pace.

"Oh, Father Konrad," Appel called out in a singsong voice. "There is something we would speak to you about."

For a moment, the old prior hitched his step and considered walking on and ignoring them. Instead, he stopped and turned reluctantly.

"Good morn to you, dear women. Now, if you will excuse me, I have an urgent matter to attend." He bobbed his head and turned to go, but Gritta managed to free her hand from Egilhard's sticky grip and snatched the prior's sleeve.

"But, my lord Prior, I think you would like to hear what we have to say. We believe we have solved the mystery of the murdered women in Colmar."

The prior looked alarmed for a moment. "What makes you think there are murdered women in Colmar?"

Appel held up a finger. "First, Hattie Jungerwald is found dead in her bed with black bruises and fingermarks around her throat. Second, Odile Lepanier drowned in a canal that is shallow enough for me to cross without wetting the hem of my skirts. Those were not accidents, Father Konrad, surely you must see."

"I know that the lords don't care what happens to the poor women of this city," Gritta said hotly, "but we do. We could be killed next."

"Indeed, for the murderer threatened Gritta only yesterday – and in her own home!" Efi interjected.

Gritta's face was grim. "It was Frau Widmer, Father. She had a reason to kill both women because she suspected them of stealing from her."

The old prior opened his mouth to speak, but Appel spoke first.

"And we saw Frau Widmer wearing the very same chemise that she claimed was stolen from her by Hattie Jungerwald, only days after Hattie was discovered dead in her house. Gritta saw Hattie purchase the linen for the chemise herself, and she was wearing the garment on the night that she died, but when I helped the nuns to prepare the body, she wore a different chemise," Appel finished triumphantly.

"Hattie and Frau Widmer had been arguing the night Hattie died. I saw it myself, and so did Girard, the night watchman. Go to him and ask for his tale if he has not told it to you already," Gritta said. "And she was bragging recently that she has money, which she could have made by selling your church treasures."

"Goodwives, return to your homes, and may the lord bless you and your families." The prior tried again to turn and leave.

"Father Konrad, we are not safe in our homes! Widmer has already killed twice, and she will do it again, especially now that she has leveled her accusation!" Gritta disentangled herself from her two children for long enough to chase the beleaguered man down the lane. A few other parishioners emerging from the church were beginning to stare and whisper amongst themselves, and the prior glanced around nervously.

"Not here, dear women, please. You are drawing attention."

"I'll draw any attention necessary to make you demand that the sheriff arrest a murderer in my neighborhood."

The prior mopped his brow. "Alright, I will not allow this woman's arrest unless she has been properly questioned, but I will send the sheriff to her home tomorrow morning, along with Friar Wikerus, to make inquiries. Will that satisfy you?"

"Yes, thank you, my lord Prior!" Appel curtseyed respectfully. "You will see – Frau Widmer is guilty. Of that I am sure. And with God's help, the truth shall come to light when she is questioned tomorrow."

One silver button

In which Frau Widmer drives a hard bargain

F RAU HILDE WIDMER HAD just finished the last of her evening chores when she felt the call of nature. Although there was a public privy nearby, the skies deposited a thin spittle of rain on her cheeks when she stepped out the door, and she quickly decided to do her business in the nearby canal so she could retreat into the warmth of her one-room house with all haste. Now that the summer heat had finally given way to cooler autumn weather, she had moved her hens and her sow with its suckling piglet inside the house. The ripe smell of animal dung was a small price to pay for the extra heat and the luxury of gathering the eggs from the comfort of her own home. Besides, it was the children's job to ensure that droppings were scooped up and tossed into the midden behind the house.

A rope of red and yellow braided wool circled her waist, serving as a girdle. From it hung a small leather pouch, her eating knife, and her measuring stick on pieces of string for easy access, and when she walked, these instruments clacked together. Her husband and children could always predict Frau

Widmer's mood by the sound and frequency of these items as they banged and tangled together. Until recently, her girdle had been a rope of rough hemp, but that was before she had come into her good fortune.

Unconsciously, Frau Widmer's hand strayed to the leather pouch and her fingers slipped past the drawstring closure, tightening around a small object within – a large silver button worth more than every object she owned inside her home. Tomorrow she would journey to Mulhouse to sell it to the Jew who lived near the goldsmith's quarter and receive silver coins in return. Perhaps, someday, she would finally amass enough to leave this stinking district and move into a house with a staircase and a sleeping floor.

She pulled her fingers back and straightened her wimple, looking back into the house. The children and her husband slept soundly on their straw mattresses, and she scowled at them for a moment. Last week, she had bought several lengths of fine, thick wool from Herr Tailleur to cover the straw, but it wasn't fine enough. She still squirmed and scratched at night. Perhaps she would use the proceeds of this button to buy herself a length of soft linen to lie upon and some herbs to mix into her straw, which would keep the fleas at bay.

With these thoughts to occupy her, Frau Widmer stepped into the dark, rainy night and cursed. There was no moon, and it was too wet and windy for a candle. She squinted down the alley behind her house, trying to decide if she wanted to brave the short walk to the canal without a lantern, and that is when she heard the squelching of heavy footsteps in the mud.

"Who goes?" she asked, her hand closing around the dull eating knife at her waist.

The footfalls stopped for a moment, then continued faster in her direction. Frau Widmer, instead of backing away, pulled the knife up higher.

"Come near me, knave, and I'll slit your throat!"

"Oh, shut up," a voice said softly. "You are so loud that you will cause all the wenches of this foul neighborhood to fling open their shutters just to see what type of performance you intend to give them tonight."

Frau Widmer deflated with relief at the familiar voice and lowered her knife.

"Why are you here? I did not hear your signal."

"That is because I hadn't a chance to give my signal. You were already outside."

"Aye, and you'd better make your business quick because I have some of my own." She crossed her legs tightly as the urge to relieve herself grew stronger.

"I have something that I need you to keep for a few days."

"Fine. That will be another button."

The figure reached into his robe and pushed something small and hard into Frau Widmer's outstretched hand. She ran her fingers over it. A button, alright, but this one was made of wood.

"What nonsense is this? I want another silver button of the same size as the last one. That's the price I charge."

"Well, I do not have more silver buttons, and I won't until I can move these items along into Strassburg." He held up a sack, and in the dull light of the moon through the clouds, she could see that it was laden with several large, heavy objects.

"Store these for me now, and after I sell them on, I will give you your button."

Frau Widmer crossed her arms over her chest. "No. I'll not do you any favors. I will help you for immediate payment only. How do I know that you won't take all your earnings and leave town for good? I'll be left with nothing."

"You'll be left with your life, you useless harpy." The robed figure stepped closer, but Frau Widmer threw back her head and laughed.

"Do you think you are the first person to threaten to kill me?"

"I certainly do not. From what I can see, the only thing stopping most of your neighbors from putting poison in your soup is the fear of hell."

"I would never let any of my neighbors near my food." Frau Widmer sniffed. "For the very reason you just gave."

"I will give you one more chance. Store these for me, and I'll pay you when there is less suspicion in the city."

"No. Silver first. Until then, you will have to find another place to hide your dirty stolen goods." The urge to relieve herself was overpowering. Frau Widmer turned to walk past the man and toward the canal. She never even felt the knife as it plunged into her back, dropping her to the ground like an alder tree.

More accused

In which the alewives find the actions of Friar Wikerus suspicious

G RITTA, APPEL AND EFI huddled together for warmth under a covered shelter to wait out the autumn rain before they continued to their homes after the morning marketing. The skies above were gray and heavy, the people below dripping and miserable. The usually boisterous market was subdued today as the shoppers only bought the essentials – turnips, cabbages, a little flour for a loaf of bread – before hurrying back to their homes and barring the doors behind them.

It had been two days since Frau Widmer was discovered in the lane behind her house with a knife thrust deep into her back. The weapon was so long and had been pushed with such force that it punctured her heart and the skin above her breast, leaving a deep red stain on her plain brown frock. Her husband, Jacques, tearfully insisted that he hadn't heard a sound, but Sheriff Werner took him to the locked cellar underneath the winemaker's guildhall anyway as a precaution so he could be questioned. Another goodwife took Frau Widmer's three pale, quiet children to help with the chores, and the dead woman's small rented house had stood cold and empty since. No one dared to go near it – even to walk past – for it was irrefutable now; a murderer roamed the streets of Colmar.

Gritta's face was downcast as she stared from their shelter at the dark windows of the Widmer house. Next to her, Efi shuffled and squirmed uncomfortably.

"I told you it was too simple of a theory to be true," Gritta muttered. "Frau Widmer was too dumb not to get caught after the first murder."

"We all knew that, but who else could we have suspected? Oh, Efi, will you stop that?" Appel snarled.

"There is something in my shoe that has been troubling my foot since we entered the market," Efi said. "I must remove it, or I will not be able to take another step." She bent over to undo the leather ties of her shoe and stopped suddenly. "Hello. What is this?"

On the ground, in the muddy indentation of her footprint, lay a carved wooden cross on a broken piece of string. Efi picked it up and held it to the light.

"This looks like a monk's cross."

"Indeed, but why would it be here?"

"Which of the brothers wears this cross?" Gritta directed the question at Appel, who was undeniably the most pious of the three of them.

"How should I know? They all wear the same cross."

The women peered into the rainy square again and searched the crowd, but no friar was nearby. Efi tugged Appel's sleeve and pointed behind them. The entrance to the lane that ran behind Frau Widmer's empty house was nearby, and it was this lane where Frau Widmer's body had been discovered. From the shelter where they stood, it would be easy for someone with ill intent to quickly dart into the lane without being seen.

"That cross looks like it hasn't been outside for long," Efi said tentatively. "Perhaps only a day or two. See, the wood isn't weathered or swollen with water, and the string isn't rotted. You don't suppose..."

Appel set her mouth in a firm line. "A man of God wouldn't. He couldn't! It is a mortal sin to take a life!"

"And it is a deadly sin also to steal from God's church, but there we have it. Someone in the prior's house could be committing both crimes."

"But why?" Efi asked. She stopped and dipped a curtsey at Hans, the butcher's son, as he swaggered by. "Oh, he is handsome, isn't he?"

"Efi! Remove your mind from that young man's breeches. We have a mystery here. It is a good question. Why would one of the brothers steal from the church and then begin killing goodwives and widows in Les Tanneurs?" Gritta asked.

It also took Appel a moment to tear her eyes from Hans' retreating figure. "Stealing the altar gold makes a bit of sense," she mused. "After all, it would be easy enough, wouldn't it? He could take the gold from the nave under the guise of prayers and then hide it quickly, moving it later when he knew the way was clear."

"Or he could even remove one of the chests where the friars store the gold. Recall that when we spoke to Friar Wikerus on the day we prayed for the souls of our dead husbands, he had been packing the gold into a chest, and he also had a key. It wouldn't be strange for a friar to be seen carrying the chest of gold since they have to move it to and from the storerooms and the reliquaries. The theft could have happened in broad daylight, in front of witnesses, and no one would be the wiser."

The rain had eased up, and the three women picked their way through the mucky street toward Gritta's house to prepare the day's pottage together, carefully hopping over the namesake ditch that gave Trench Lane its name. After days of rain, the ditch was a roaring torrent of stinking brown water.

Inside the house, Efi and Appel filled the pot with well-water and stoked the fire while Gritta tended to her twins, Anstett and Mattheus, who had managed to tie their thumbs together with a length of hempen string. The two little thumbs were turning purple, and Mattheus wailed with pain. Next to him, Anstett was philosophical about the situation.

"Man cannot live without his thumbs, Mother," the little boy said solemnly. "I know this now in a way that I did not understand before."

"But how did you manage to tie your thumbs in knots without using both of your thumbs?!" Gritta scolded as she worked at the string.

"Lonel tied them for us."

When she had managed to loosen the string and liberate her twins, she ripped the door open, her eyes wild. Lonel was running in the rain toward the nearest alleyway. Gritta shook her fist at his retreating back.

"That's right, run, you scourge! What am I supposed to do with two thumbless sons, I ask you? Why don't you make yourself useful and go find my hoe!"

"Your hoe is still lost?" Appel asked, inspecting the purpling appendages of both boys. "They'll be fine, Gritta." And she slipped each boy a small oatcake. "These ought to help your thumbs feel better," she whispered to them.

Gritta sat heavily on a bench. "Aye, my hoe is still lost. What am I going to do, Appel? Jorges takes all of the earnings from the brewin', and these children are going to be the death of me. Lisette is a wanton woman, and Lonel was dragged home by the night watchman yesterday because he was trying to ride Herr Volker's sheep."

"Every boy tries to ride the sheep at some point, Gritta." Appel patted her friend's hand.

"Aye, but he dressed the sheep first in my finest frock. Herr Volker thought that Lonel was messing with his daughter, for the light was dim. Lonel has a fine bruise from where Herr Volker struck him."

A loud knock sounded at the door. Efi jumped up to answer it, and they could hear the genial, booming voice of Friar Wikerus.

"In the name of heaven, will that man ever stop visiting at the worst time? It's as if he has a nose for disaster," Gritta mumbled, wiping away a stray tear.

Efi ushered Friar Wikerus into the room, and he greeted the twins cordially, inspecting their now bright-red thumbs with all the clinical seriousness of a barber-surgeon. When the boys had scampered from the room, he turned his attention to Gritta and Appel.

"My dear goodwives, it is almost beyond my comprehension that I am here for a third time to console you on the loss of a dear friend and neighbor."

Gritta's eyes narrowed, and she snatched Appel's hand in an iron grip.

"I did not know Frau Widmer well, but I understand that she was your neighbor for many years, and you must feel her loss keenly," he continued.

"No, Friar Wikerus, not in any particular way," Appel said.

"Indeed, I can now work undisturbed by her constant accusations and gossip," said Gritta. Both women looked at Friar Wikerus with iron gazes, and he suddenly felt the need to stand and edge his plump frame toward the door.

"Well, it seems I misunderstood your friendship with the poor woman. I urge you to comfort and care for her widowed husband and dear children until he can remarry and to pray for her soul in church when you are there next."

Gritta stood and drew herself up to her full stature, which had been buxom in her younger years before the Great

Pestilence. Nevertheless, she still thrust out her significantly lowered chest and squared her shoulders, her eyes commanding attention with their half-lowered lids and piercing blue stare.

"When Frau Odile was murdered in Les Tanneurs, you were at Frau Appel's door in less than a day. What took you so long this time, Friar?"

Friar Wikerus favored them with a perplexed smile. "Well, I have been very preoccupied lately with the thefts of the altar gold. Did you not hear that the prior has assigned me to work with the sheriff to determine the culprit?"

"Aye, we did."

"Well, at the same time that our poor Frau Widmer was being stabbed, some foul knave was also stealing the altar gold again – the candlesticks that you observed upon your visit to the church to pray for your deceased husbands." He nodded to Appel and Efi.

"How terrible for you and the prior," Gritta said flatly, crossing her arms. Friar Wikerus backed away another pace toward the door and reached for the handle.

"Well, I can see you are busy, so I shall leave you to your womanly work."

"Womanly work?" Gritta shot the remark at him like a stone from a sling. "Chopping wood, banking fires, and untying hostage thumbs is womanly work?"

Now Friar Wikerus looked genuinely uncomfortable, and Gritta felt a rush of satisfaction. Let the holy man squirm, she thought.

"All work is womanly work, Friar. We do it all, but our husbands receive the accolades for it."

"Whatever do you mean, goodwife Gritta?"

"Take, for example, my husband, Jorges. At one time a godly man, and a handsome one too, Jorges even used to fetch the water from the well in the mornings, though the other women would tease him. He would laugh and say, 'It's for my love, and how can I tell her no?' And then the children came. First Lisette, and then Michel and Geld, and then Noe. Suddenly, Jorges was not around as often, and I had to fetch my own water from the well, despite being burdened with four young'uns."

Appel nodded sagely next to her. Gritta continued, her voice raising an octave.

"Margaret, Lonel, Rosmunda, Urbe; babies came and came, and why? Because Jorges was insatiable. But every time a new one came, Jorges would spend more time away from the house, and I took on more work. I chopped the wood and brought it into the house. I slaughtered the pigs and scalded them myself. When the roof fell in, and we didn't have the coin to pay the thatcher, I climbed aloft myself and shored up the holes with straw that I cut from the field myself. And where was Jorges?"

By now, Friar Wikerus looked distinctly uncomfortable. He had a hand resting on the handle of the door, and his entire body angled toward it, ready to flee.

"Jorges was in Vogelgrun, occasionally working and spending all of his coin on drink before he arrived home! It was a lovely living for Jorges, who felt unencumbered by his family whenever he was away, but not so lovely for me. So I ask you, what is 'women's work,' truly?"

"God says wives are to submit to their husbands," Friar Wikerus replied weakly and winced as Appel and Efi stood up next to her.

"Tell me, Friar Wikerus," Gritta asked coldly. "What happened to your wooden cross? You wear it so often that it seems quite unnatural to see you without your holy adornment."

Wikerus's hand wandered to his chest, clutching at the bare spot where his wooden cross should have hung. Gritta's eyes narrowed further.

"Indeed, it has been missing for a day now. I confess I am at quite a loss to say where it went. I applaud your skill of observation, Frau Gritta, for noticing that it was missing."

"You must be devastated to have lost it, Friar." Gritta's voice was thick with sarcasm. "You are a holy man, after all, and the cross is your calling." She only broke her iron stare when Appel pinched her on her rump to stop her talking.

By now, Friar Wikerus had the door cracked open and edged most of his body through the doorframe and into the damp late-autumn afternoon. He forced a smile and bowed quickly.

"Alewives, I can see that you are handling the tragedy of Frau Widmer's death admirably and require no assistance from me. Please do let me know if there is anything you require. I can be found, as always, with the Dominican brothers if you need me." He dashed outside and hurried into the square, with Gritta following him. She remained on her stoop, arms crossed and glaring until he was out of sight.

Suspects

In which Gritta proposes her theory

GRITTA RETURNED TO HER house, slamming the door behind her. "Good riddance, and God is great," she mumbled. Appel and Efi both watched her with stony faces.

"Why did you do that, Gritta?" Appel yelled. "There is nothing to be gained by acting like a sour old wench when the man was just trying to comfort us during our hardship. I thought you were a wise woman, but you acted like a high-spirited maid with no interest in being civil!"

"Oh, poor Friar Wikerus!" Efi cried.

Gritta threw up her hands and shooed her remaining children from the house. When the three of them were alone, she sat on a bench with a board on her lap and calmly began to slice some leeks for the pottage.

"Tell me, girls," Gritta asked, punctuating her sentence with a particularly savage chop from her iron knife. "What do you think happened to the wooden cross that Friar Wikerus wears?"

"It is as he said. He lost it." Appel picked up a bowl of barley and began to sort it, tossing the straws and stones into the crackling fire.

Gritta nodded patiently. "And did we find anything unusual in the market this morning?"

Efi slowly withdrew the wooden cross on the broken string from the small purse tied to her girdle. "You don't suppose it could have been him, do you? I don't seek out his company, but surely Friar Wikerus has always been considerate to us."

"Perhaps too considerate, Efi," Gritta said as she swept the leeks into the pot with a swift movement of her knife.

"Are you suggesting that Friar Wikerus may have been watching us, trying to decide if we were to be his next victims?" Appel asked, aghast.

"He does seem to spend a lot of time in Les Tanneurs, and with us."

"He is just doing his duty to the community. As a Franciscan and a member of a mendicant order, he is commanded to be out among the people," Appel offered weakly. "He will probably move on soon to Riquewihr or Ribeauville."

"Appel, his carved wooden cross is gone from its thong about his neck, and he has not replaced it. What kind of Franciscan would allow such a thing to happen? He should have replaced it immediately. And besides, Efi discovered it directly across the square from the site of Frau Widmer's murder. It is clear that at some time during the last two days, Friar Wikerus was standing beneath that shelter."

Efi and Appel nodded miserably.

"That makes him a suspect of Frau Widmer's death in my mind."

Appel jumped to her feet and shoved the unoccupied benches from the center of the room, commanding the space like a minstrel on a stage. "Right then. Girls, we must make some sense of this. Let us review what we know."

"We have a carved wooden cross that looks as if it came from one of the Dominican brothers," Efi said.

"But we don't know which brother. It could have been Wikerus, or it could have been a different friar."

"It was Wikerus because his cross was missing, and he had no reasonable explanation for its absence." Gritta crossed her arms. "You saw him stammer and hesitate when I asked him about it."

Appel nodded and continued. "Here is what else we know. We know that Wikerus visited us after the previous two deaths."

"And he did it immediately," Efi chirped.

"Indeed, so why did he wait so long this time?"

"Because he knew this time that it was impossible to convince Sheriff Werner the death in Les Tanneurs was not murder," Gritta said. "Hattie was strangled, but only Appel noticed the marks of fingers on her throat. Odile drowned in the canal, but there's no way to prove it wasn't an accident. However, it's impossible to believe that a knife found its own way into Frau Widmer's back."

"We also know that Friar Wikerus ordered a subordinate friar in the priory to sit underneath the church's altar and wait for a thief to try and steal the altar gold."

"But no gold was stolen."

Appel nodded. "Indeed. And since he is the prior's investigator, this would put him in a protected position. He could have set the trap as a ruse to try and make it look like he was hunting the thief, giving him the opportunity to point the accusatory finger at someone else – in this case, Frau Henninga."

"Who also happens to be a poor widow," Gritta offered.

"Frau Widmer may have caught him, and he paid for her silence. Even a newcomer like him knew that she was a ruthless busybody. That explains why she was bragging about having money."

"But what about Hattie and Odile?" Efi asked, and for a moment, all three women were silent in their own thoughts.

"Perhaps they knew his secret? Perhaps they knew he was the thief," Efi said.

"Or perhaps he is no friar, and he just likes to kill," Gritta hissed. "I have heard of such men. Like the armies of King Charles, they roam the countryside and destroy wherever they go. Perhaps he is a rogue knight? Don't forget that he is a newcomer to Colmar. How much does Father Konrad really know about Friar Wikerus? Is he even a holy man or just an evil knave in disguise?"

For a moment, the women considered the pleasant countenance and rotund figure of Friar Wikerus clad in a knight's armor, a sword dripping with blood at his side as he mopped his tonsured brow with a handkerchief.

"That man is no knight," Appel said. Gritta and Efi quickly agreed.

By now, the light was failing, and Appel looked outside the unshuttered window with apprehension.

"My dears, I must return to my home, and Efi, yours is furthest away from us. Allow me to escort you back."

Efi nodded mutely, and Gritta saw them to the edge of the square before hurrying back into her own home, where her children were now beginning to assemble. Rosmunda was spreading a freshly washed blanket over the straw mattress, and Urbe ladled scoops of pottage onto thick slabs of stale bread for Anstett and Mattheus, who were relating the story of their captured thumbs in exaggerated terms. Even Lonel had returned, steaming slightly in his rain-soaked clothes as he lounged near the fire.

Gritta smiled, shut the door behind her, and joined them.

Charitable, honest, kind, and hardworking

In which a sleeping arrangement is made out of necessity

"Appel, I think you should sleep with me tonight," Efi said as the older woman prepared a small oil lamp to escort Efi home. "It is not safe in this neighborhood."

"And what about Gritta?"

"I also worry about Frau Gritta, but she has eight children living at home with her and a husband besides. All the murders occurred within a short distance of your house and in the nighttime, so I think you should come with me and stay as my bedfellow until it is safe."

Appel did not particularly feel like leaving her house. The mash tuns, which quietly burped their now familiar odor of yeasty fermentation, were a comfort to her. The weather would soon grow colder, and she would move her hens upstairs to a more comfortable part of the house, with more space and two windows to let the light through. But three women had been murdered in her very neighborhood. It was no longer possible to ignore the danger to her, a woman living alone. She grudgingly agreed, on the condition that they could return to her house at first light to ensure that the thieves hadn't gotten inside and made off with her best cup, a copper chalice given as a wedding gift.

As the two widows walked carefully toward Efi's house, they encountered the sheriff and Girard, the night watchman. Both held shielded lanterns on long poles to light their way through the darkened streets.

"Frau Appel, Frau Efi," Sheriff Werner growled. "I don't like you being out so late in the streets. Girard is here to help me enforce the curfew this evening, seeing as the deaths in this part of city have all occurred in the darkness. I want no one out of their homes after sunset unless it is to fetch the surgeon or use the privy. Only me, Girard, and Friar Wikerus may roam at night."

"Why is Friar Wikerus allowed to be out at night?" Efi asked.

"Because he has to keep a wary eye out for the thief of the church's treasures. It's not easy being a man in Colmar right now, I'll tell you that. We have to keep a wary eye for anything suspicious. Always on our guard. You women have it easy because we're here to protect you and keep the peace."

Efi and Appel looked at each other for a moment.

"Well," Appel said, "we'll just be going, then. I am to sleep with Efi until the murderer is found. Because we don't have any of those brave men to watch over us, it falls to us to watch ourselves, seeing as only women are dying in Les Tanneurs."

She turned and stomped into the darkness with Efi trotting at her heels.

"The nerve of that man! The cheek!" Appel fumed.

"He does show a considerable slowness of mind and baseness of language," Efi commented, nodding her head.

At Efi's little house on the other side of the city walls, the two women lay on their backs on a mattress of fresh straw, staring at the dark ceiling while the light of the dying fire flickered on the walls.

"Appel," Efi whispered. "You don't really believe that Friar Wikerus could be guilty, do you? He seems such a nice young man. So genuine."

Appel took a while to answer, and in the darkness, all Efi could see was the reflection of the firelight in her eyes as she stared sightlessly into the dark.

"I loved a man once who was charitable, honest, kind, and hardworking – just like my own papa. I was going to marry him. He had even spoken to my father. Papa had a bit of land put by for me, and so we had plans to build a house upon it. He was a tradesman, my love was. A pewterer, fast on his way to joining the guild."

Efi sat up and leaned on her elbow, wide awake. "But I thought your husband was a tanner?"

Appel nodded. "My betrothed had promised to sup with my family and me on the eve before the wedding. When he didn't arrive and the sun began to set, I worried, so my papa went out looking for him. He returned without my betrothed, and that's when he told me that he had found my lover in the arms of another woman and driven him out of town. The next morning the whole square was talking about it. I spent my youth in Les Canaux, not in Les Tanneurs, you see."

In the darkness, Efi put a consoling hand on Appel's arm. Appel continued to stare at the ceiling.

"His shame shall follow him even after death, Appel. He will have to account for his infidelity before God!" Efi said.

But Appel shook her head slowly. "It was a lie," she whispered. "My betrothed did not come to the house to sup because that very morning, my papa had tied him up, placed him on a wine cart to Strassburg, and warned him upon pain of death to never show his face in Colmar again. The story about finding my lover in the arms of another was false. My papa, whom everyone thought a good man, faked his search, returned, and lied to me. He broke my heart and got to keep what he wanted."

"How did you find out the truth?"

"The cart that Papa used to drive my betrothed from town belonged to Adolphus Schlock, the father of Johannes Schlock, who now owns the weinstube. He confessed everything to me. Told me that my father didn't want to part with the land, nor with the extra hands at the house to tend to his wool washing business."

"And then what happened?"

"And then I became angry. I met my husband, Giles, a tanner's son, and lay with him. When my belly began to swell, and I could no longer hide it, my father was forced to make us marry and to give up the land owed to me."

"And then you were trapped with the tanner until he died?" Efi asked, her eyes wide.

Appel smiled and rolled over to face the younger woman on the crackling straw mattress. "Not trapped. I loved Giles, too. I might have married him in anger, but we lived in love, and even though I was a tanner's wife, I was happy. But I always wondered what happened to Laurent, my betrothed. I always wondered why he didn't return and take me away from my father's house. I lay awake at nights, wishing he would kidnap me and take me with him."

"Appel, I am grieved to hear of your lost lover."

"Both of them were considered good men, like Friar Wikerus," Appel whispered. "But both used me poorly. My tanner may have been lower in their eyes and not always on his best behavior, but he always did right by me, and I miss him."

For a moment, the only sound in the room was the dry hiss from the cooling embers in the fire. Appel's eyes began to close slowly, and Efi snuggled close to her, pleased to be sleeping with another body after a long, lonely summer without her husband.

Suddenly, a loud banging on the door jolted them awake, and they both sat up straight on the mattress. Appel looked to her right, snatched up a long spindle with a stone on its base, and thrust it into Efi's hands.

"Efi, I shall open the door. You stand behind me with your spindle, and if whoever is on the other side of the door tries to lunge at me, you shall strike him over the head while I scream for help, do you understand?"

"Y-yes!" Efi was quivering in her gray wool chemise. Appel grabbed the still-empty chamber pot and held it aloft over her head in a white-knuckled hand as she unbarred the door and cracked it open with the other.

"That's the twelfth bell!" a voice bellowed from outside. "Smother your fire or risk burning the whole city to ashes!"

Appel lowered her chamber pot. "It's only Girard, the night watchman," she told Efi. "Be gone, Girard. We were just about to put the fire out."

"Apologies, Herr Girard, we were talking too late into the night." Efi curtseyed.

Girard lowered his pole-held lantern and peered into the dark room at Efi. "Here now, you women aren't getting up to anything sinful, are you?"

Appel drew herself up. "Girard of Eguisheim, get you to Saint Martin's church to have your filthy mind cleansed! How dare you insinuate such a thing about me and the widow Efi, who invited me to stay at her house for the sake of my welfare. We are two poor women trying to protect each other."

Girard shrugged his shoulders, and Appel noted an expression of mild disappointment cloud his rough features. She supposed if she had confessed to illicit deeds with Efi, Girard would have had fuel for his imagination during his lonely nights on watch.

"Well, stifle that fire straightaway. I have more rounds to make, and I don't want to come back here after I circle the walls and find that you haven't put it out. One ember! That's all it takes to set an entire city alight!" He held a stubby finger aloft, then turned and marched into the gloom until all that was visible was a ball of light hovering in the air from his lantern.

Appel took up a small rake and spread the coals so they would smother, while Efi straightened the bedding. Then the two women, one older and aching for her lost daughter and husband, the other young and full of insecurities, fell asleep in each other's arms.

Arrests

In which the alewives are distracted by their own incarceration

NO WOMEN WERE MURDERED that night in Colmar. And no women were murdered the night after or the one after that. Days went by, and the residents of Colmar began to relax as Frau Widmer's grisly murder faded from their collective memory. As winter approached on swift, chilly feet, the fields sparkled in the morning sun with a thin layer of frost – a reminder to everyone in the valley that inadequate preparation for the coldest months meant death.

On those early winter mornings, Appel's empty house always felt damp and lonely when she and Efi arrived to light the fire in the hearth to start the day's brewing. Frau Widmer's murder may not be foremost in the minds of the burghers and merchants any longer, but to the alewives, the threat was still real, and Appel continued to stay with Efi in the nights.

Every day, while they paced around the house a hundred and twelve circles to time the soaking of the gruit, they would discuss their theories about the murders and the thefts at the church. The more they talked, the more convinced Gritta was that Friar

Wikerus had the opportunity and the motivation to commit the crimes.

"Why will you two not believe me," Gritta shouted one day as Appel and Efi hesitated after another of her evidence-laden tirades.

"It's just...he's a man of the church. And he is kind to us. Your argument is sound, Gritta, but my heart won't believe it," Efi said. "And Frau Appel doesn't, neither."

Gritta sighed. "Who else could it be, girls? No one else has the opportunity or the motivation. And what about the cross that Efi found? Will you truly wait for him to come and take your lives next?"

"Even if he is guilty, Gritta, what can we do? He has friends in high places," Appel whispered. "We are powerless."

Gritta set her jaw and crossed her arms. "I'll think of something, mark me. He can't get away with murder in my city."

Efi was the strongest because of her youth, so she set about early each morning to fetch water from Herr Gerhard's stream. Gritta would prepare the barley for malting, sifting it through a willow sieve to remove weevils, pebbles, and other grit, while Appel provided a supervisory role, citing her age and wisdom as qualities that were equally important to the process of brewing ale.

"You might at least help carry the pots into the souring corner," Gritta grumbled one day as she tried to roll the ponderously heavy tuns into the darkest and coolest corner of the house for the fermentation to begin.

"At my age? Imagine what that would do to these old bones!" Appel set her knitting down to illustrate her offense.

Gritta straightened and massaged her lower back with her thumbs. "If what I know about you is true, your old bones are capable of more than you let on."

"Well, I think it's time that I feed my hens." Appel jumped to her feet and swept into the icy dooryard where five speckled chickens scratched at the frozen earth amongst the leafless grape vines.

Gritta chuckled and grasped another tun, bracing her feet and readying herself to pull it forward. The light in the room dimmed, and she looked up to find the doorway blocked with men, and Sheriff Werner at the head of them. She heard a shout and glanced out the window. One man held Appel by the arm while another wrenched the waterskins from Efi's hands as she protested loudly. Sheriff Werner straightened his shoulders and cleared his throat with authority.

"Frau Gritta, I require you to come with me. The city council wishes to speak with you and your friends."

"What nonsense are you on about, Sheriff? Can't you see we're busy here?"

Behind the sheriff, she heard one of the men mutter dangerously to another. They were peering behind him into the house as if they expected to see a wild animal come running out of it.

"Come without a fuss now, and don't make a scene for your neighbors to gossip about, Gritta." The sheriff took her arm and led her out of the house. "All of you are to be tried in front of a group of your peers before sentencing."

"Tried for what and sentencing of whom?!" Appel had managed to free her arm and drew herself up to her full, regal height, which was taller than two out of the three men.

The sheriff cleared his throat. "It has come to our attention that you three women are brewing ale and selling it at the inns and merchant houses."

"And what is wrong with that?" Appel demanded.

"You can ask more questions when we reach the council."

Efi's eyes filled with tears. "But..."

"That's enough now, Frau Efi. You may be pretty and innocent, but your punishment will be the same as these other two women, who know better than to lead a younger woman down the path of sin. Their shame shall be to see you suffer along with them."

"The path of sin? What are you talking about, you clod?" Gritta shouted.

"Quiet. You can explain to the council."

"But we found your murderer and the thief of the altar gold! We discovered who killed Hattie, Odile, and Frau Widmer, and he is right in front of your own bulbous noses!" Gritta poked a finger in the direction of the Dominican church.

"All I see are three women behaving in an arrogant manner, women who assume that they know more about investigating a murder than I do. Well, God elevated me to my position so that I might keep order and peace in this city, not you three, and the council thinks you're threatening that peace. Now let's go."

The "council" was a huddle of men who gathered beneath a thatched pavilion held up by sturdy pine posts and open to the air. Rain had begun to drizzle down, and the wind blew in sideways through the pavilion so that, in a few moments, everyone was soaked and shivering.

"Why must they hold this infernal council outside when there is room at the inn with a warm hearth and benches to sit? Even a drafty church would be better," Appel grumbled as two men led her by the arms. Next to her, Efi wailed as she was led into the pavilion, and Gritta's face was a mask of grim fury.

The women were all told to stand while the councilmen sat on narrow wooden benches facing them. Then the sheriff stood and cleared his throat.

"Well men, thank you all for coming." He shuffled his feet. "I received word that these three accused were working in defiance of the natural order and decided to investigate for myself. I looked through the window of Frau Appel's house one day, and it was evident to me that there is a large brewing effort happening there. This brewing goes beyond what one woman will need for herself and a bit of extra to sell. She has removed all furnishings to make way for mash tuns, and her fire smokes day and night to boil water and malt barley."

"Defiance? Defiance of what?" Appel demanded.

"You ain't payin' no taxes on your wares, wenches!" a toothless old merchant shouted. "We asked, and no one has sold you a leaf of gruit."

"And there are also the rumors that the widow Appel has tried her hand at witchcraft," Herr Hervé, the clothmaker, chirped. "Another reason to question them. She could be corrupting the other two!"

Appel hung her head and sighed heavily. The rumors, once started, never seemed to go away.

"It's in defiance of the natural order of things," the sheriff interrupted. "Your menfolk can sell to the merchants in the villages, but you must not do work that puts you outside of God's plan for a woman."

"What plan is that?" Gritta asked. "Is this his plan?" She pointed to the yellowing bruises on her face. Although it was a month since Jorges had struck her, the pain and discoloration persisted.

"Well, uh…" The sheriff shuffled his feet again and looked at his hands.

Another councilman, old and trembling, stood and waved his stick at Gritta.

"I heard that Jorges gave his wife that mark as a reminder to be a chaste woman. First brewing, and then what next? Whorin'? Saying incantations to the Devil like some infidel?! One sin leads to another!"

Herr Hervé, the clothmaker, nodded vigorously. He was the youngest of the council, and rarely did anyone allow him to utter a word during trials.

"He hit me because he was selling the ale that we brewed and then stealing our coin. And he don't like admitting it!" Gritta screamed, pounding her fist on the pine-trunk pillar that held up the structure. A light rain of weevils and dust graced the heads of the assembled. "And where is my dear husband, anyway?" Gritta's voice was thick with sarcasm. "I do not see him here?"

"Here he is, Frau Gritta!" a voice called out, and two men approached, holding Jorges up by the scruff of his tunic. "We found him inside Frau Appel's house, drinking straight from the ale tun like a horse at a trough."

Jorges smiled lopsidedly and bowed to the crowd from between his two human props. "And a good day to all of you," he slurred. He glanced at Gritta and grinned. "Ah, my fair bride! What happened to your face?"

"You spawn of Satan!" Gritta roared. "The Devil take you back to where you came from!"

It took two men to hold Gritta back as she lunged at Jorges. All the while, as she was screaming her outrage, Jorges continued to grin. One of the men holding him up slapped his cheeks a few times.

"Jorges," he whispered. "Your wife's on trial!"

"Trial? Why?"

"Brewing and saying incantations. Selling ale to the shops instead of to the goodwives of the city, like she ought to be doin'."

"Ah." Jorges nodded enthusiastically. "That she is."

Next to them, Efi wailed even louder.

"Silence!" the sheriff shouted above the din. "Now, we're here to determine the punishment for these three. They are defying the natural order. If these three alewives wish to sell their excess brew, no one will challenge them. After all, many women of the city brew and sell their excess. But none of them—" the sheriff held up a finger, and all movement in the room stopped "—none of those goodwives of the city are making ale in the quantity of these three. Why, they sold twelve barrels to Karl Gastwirt. Now, twelve barrels is enough to make a proper profit, and do you think these women will be wise with their money? Surely not. They behave like men by brewing and selling their wares in such excess and then hide behind their womanhood."

Around the shelter, the men turned and nodded, for each man knew that if these three began to profit from such an ale operation, there would be no stopping the other goodwives of Colmar.

"Who knows what other things they may be doing, the three of them, that defy nature," Sheriff Werner said darkly, and the assembled jury of men glanced at each other, some with horror on their faces and some with a sort of excited curiosity. "What shall their punishment be?"

"Whipping with a willow twig!" one man yelled.

Another jumped to his feet. "The pillory!"

"How about we let them continue to brew and sell, only without the help of Jorges Leporteur?" a new voice casually called out, and everyone turned to see who had spoken.

"A man of God never interferes..."

In which a man of God interferes

FRIAR WIKERUS SMILED SERENELY and walked forward among the councilmen. Behind him, two of Karl Gastwirt's young assistants rolled a rundlet each of ale to the front of the crowd where the three women stood.

"I've just arrived home from Strassburg this very morning. I was on a visit to a dear friend who resides at the Cathedral of Notre Dame." At his words, Appel and two of the councilmembers crossed themselves and looked heavenward for a moment. Only once had Appel seen the grand cathedral in the bishopric of Strassburg, and she was never the same after. Friar Wikerus nodded his head in acknowledgment of their piety.

"Upon arriving back in Colmar, I searched for Sheriff Werner to discuss some new ideas about our altar gold thief, but alas, I could find him nowhere. After some investigation, I learned that you were all meeting to form a jury. Now, a man of God generally does not interfere with the realm of mortal laws if he is not required to, but I was curious. You see," and here he motioned to Karl Gastwirt's assistants, who lifted the rundlets to a bench and drilled a hole in each with an auger. "While in Strassburg, I was curious about the local ale, so I brought a cask home with me. I thought a taste test might be a worthy experiment. I am sure you must all be thirsty after so much yelling."

From inside his robe, Friar Wikerus produced a copper dipper with a flourish. "Straight from the prior's cellars," he announced. "We usually use it for wine, you must understand, but I thought his prized dipper could be useful today. Come now, men, please line up to take your refreshment."

The men all looked at each other for a moment, then sheepishly formed a line. Nearby, Appel, Efi, and Gritta glanced at each other.

The men made their way through the line, drinking a dipper from one cask and then a dipper from the other before retreating to their benches. A genial hum of conversation and good-natured ribbing rose from their ranks as the ale went to their heads. Friar Wikerus also partook, and when he raised his dipper in salute to the three women and winked, they all looked back at him miserably. Finally, Friar Wikerus held his hands above his head to signal for silence.

"Now, friends! Which of the two ales did you think tasted better? The one served by Erland here, or the one served by Klint?"

"Erland!" they shouted. "Erland's ale is the finest!"

Friar Wikerus nodded sagely. "Aye, Erland is in possession of the best ale, I agree. And why is that? It's fresher and made with the best water in all of Alsace! And do you know where that water comes from?"

The men looked at each other, bewildered.

"It comes from Colmar," he answered for them. "'Tis the cleanest and is supplied from the brooks that bubble from the earth at the foot of the great Kayserberg itself. And what is more, the specific stream that provides the water for this brew runs past the church, imbuing it with blessing." He looked heavenward for a moment, and several men followed his example, raising their eyes reverently toward the pavilion's roof. "The ale that Brother Klint served..." he paused for dramatic effect, "is from Strassburg, using water from the canals where the people and the dogs both piss, no doubt. It's what you've been drinking in your inns and taverns because no alewife in this city has the means to brew beyond what she can provide for her own household." Friar Wikerus paused again. "And if my own personal survey of the area is correct, one in four of the breweries in Strassburg is managed and operated by women."

The sheriff cleared his throat. "Ah, but a woman can indeed place a green branch outside of her house and invite guests to pay for an ale, but what we have here—" he pointed at the three alewives "—is a house full of cauldrons and barrels that rivals an alewerks you would find even in Amsterdam."

Friar Wikerus nodded. "And so in Strassburg. The brewsters of that fair city have minds for commerce and how to run their alewerks, and so do these alewives here."

The men now began to talk amongst themselves. Eventually, a well-dressed man, one of the free peasants of the village and a respected elder, stood.

"So, this fine ale of theirs comes from the waters of your priory? How do Jorges and these three women have access to that brook? Even the miller petitioned Father Konrad for the use of the water and was denied."

"They have special permission from the prior."

At this, Appel, Gritta, and Efi all looked at Brother Wikerus, shocked. If they had permission, they were not aware of it.

"Did you get the water from the priorywhen the men arrested you today?" Appel whispered to Efi.

"No! I got it from Herr Gerhard's brook, as you instructed, because of your arrangement with him." Efi turned to Appel. "What kind of arrangement do you have with Herr Gerhard, anyway?"

"Hush!"

"So," Friar Wikerus asked in a loud voice. "Do you want to drink the ale from Strassburg or the ale from the holiest, cleanest water in Colmar?"

The men glanced around at each other. "Colmar!" one of them shouted, and the others raised their voices in agreement. "Let the alewives of Strassburg keep their piss water for their own citizens!" one man shouted. Another jumped to his feet.

"I propose we drink only the ale of our city and no one else's!"

From where he stood, still supported by two strong young men, Jorges added his slurred agreement to the shouts from the now tipsy councilmen. The sheriff clapped his hands loudly for attention.

"Men!" he shouted. "We were not drawn here by our stomachs! We came because we must determine if these women sinned."

Brother Wikerus's expression darkened and he rolled up his wide, woolen sleeves.

"Yes, Sheriff," he said, a glint in his bright blue eyes. "Let us all talk about sin."

All the gold in church

In which Friar Wikerus feels triumph and despair in the same day

A PPEL, GRITTA, AND EFI walked slowly through the damp streets alongside Friar Wikerus, who had Jorges' arm slung over his shoulders. Jorges had better use of his legs but still swayed precariously as his knees buckled every now and again. The prospect of Jorges falling headlong into a canal and dying of injury or drowning was always possible, and the man of God didn't feel like administering the last rites on this day. Friar Wikerus was exhausted from the ordeal.

The three alewives were all somber and quiet, still hanging their heads, and Gritta's drooped with the most penitence, for she now found herself in the debt of Friar Wikerus, the man she had accused of being a murderer. Worse, she now doubted her assessment of his guilt.

As soon as Sheriff Werner mentioned the sinfulness of women during the trial, Friar Wikerus set off on a fiery sermon about hypocrisy and the Lord's judgment for unfaithfulness. Wikerus knew from the confessions he'd heard and the cherry-red complexion of several of the council members that his words had struck a nerve with them.

"Who of you," he asked them, "are innocent of the sin of lust? Who of the sin of fornication, even if only fornication in your mind's eye? Who of you is more blameless than these women or the thief in the church?"

The only reply was the screech of the wind as it howled through the thatched shelter. Sheriff Werner had chosen the outdoor pavilion to keep the three women cold and off their guard, but now he and the rest of the council were feeling distinctly uncomfortable themselves. Wikerus had jabbed a finger in the direction of the alewives, his eyes blazing. "You waste your time trying to punish these women for trying to keep food in their bellies, when we have a thief and a murderer walking free around our city!" And now he looked at each man in turn, letting his gaze linger on every face. "Why, one of you men could be the culprit. This 'trial' seems like a good way to distract the sheriff and me from our work, which is to catch these two evil knaves who are killing and stealing from God himself."

Although he knew it was a sin to feel pride in oneself, Wikerus smiled discreetly as he walked in the street. He'd always had a talent for sermon. He enjoyed the way his words had affected the men of the council. To make peace and ensure their future cooperation, he had offered the rundlets of ale to the council members, but they grumbled, demurred, and scattered into the streets to return to their wives and homes.

Jorges hummed a little tune now, swinging his hands along to the rhythm. "Come, Gritta my love, sing with me like you used to!" he slurred.

Gritta shot Jorges a look that could have killed him faster than a sword.

"You must learn to forgive him, Gritta," Friar Wikerus said quietly. "And help your husband recover from his affliction of the drink."

Gritta's eyes watered. "He never used to be like this, Friar. But after the pestilence, he had to drink to sleep at night. We could hear our neighbors wailing for their loved ones or crying out in terror when they discovered their own illness. That was how he saw himself through it."

"And how did you see yourself through it, Frau Gritta?"

Gritta stared straight ahead in the dimming twilight. "Didn't have no time for crying or drinking. I had ten babies to tend. Ten mouths to feed and to keep safe from the pestilence. I birthed those fiends, and nothing will take them off this earth unless it is my own hand."

Jorges stumbled, and Wikerus propped him up again. "We all need to find a way to gain peace, especially now, Frau Gritta. What happened to those of us who survived was terrifying. Seek solace in God's word—"

"No."

The friar's pace hesitated. Behind them, Appel had her arm around Efi, who still sniffled into her sleeve, her tears finally abating after their ordeal. Gritta jerked her chin back at her friends.

"They are where I find solace, Friar. Those who are here on earth, caring for me. Those who lived, not a God who allowed the pestilence to strike us down."

"Now, Frau Gritta—"

"I will go to your church when required, and I will say the words you tell me to say, but I will not find solace in them."

"There is power in God, Gritta. If I had told the council that the water for your brew came from Herr Gerhard's stream, the men would have immediately become suspicious, and you would have been at risk of punishment." He briefly glanced back at Appel. "But when I told them that the water for the brew came from the stream near the priory, it immediately became holy water in their minds. The mere mention of such a thing completely changed their perception of what you women are doing. All it took was the power of God."

"That is not God's power; that is your power to exploit those men with your words."

Gritta's response stung. Wikerus had been guilty in the past of questioning the validity of God, but once he learned to use the words to sway people, he no longer considered their truth. And he did not want to consider it now.

"I will pray for you, Frau Gritta."

They had arrived at Gritta's door, and inside she could see that a fire flickered in the hearth and Rosmunda moved about the large trestle table, judiciously putting her younger brothers to work while she stirred the cooking pot and wiped the cups and trenchers with a cloth. Anstett, who was only four summers old, cried alone in a corner, and the twins sat still and silent with their heads down.

"That city council has gone and terrified my children. Imagine them learning that their mother was dragged away by the sheriff." Gritta crossed her arms and glowered at Friar Wikerus.

Jorges jerked his head up and gasped in delight upon finding himself outside his threshold. He tripped into the house. "Children, I have returned!" he shouted, and Anstett ran to him.

Gritta looked straight at Friar Wikerus. "I am grateful to you for your help, Friar. I'll admit, I was convinced that you stole the gold and killed the women of Les Tanneurs, but now I believe you to be an honest man. And as an honest man, you must help us. Hattie, Odile, and even Frau Widmer need to rest in their graves. We must find their killer."

Friar Wikerus hurried back to the church. The rain had long since stopped, but the hem of his robe was caked in mud nonetheless. If he hurried, he might have time to change into a clean robe and be down to the chapel in time for Vespers. His short journey to see his friend and counselor, Father Anselmo, in Strassburg had been a balm to his soul, but the good Father hadn't managed to provide any helpful advice on what to do about the stolen altar gold. Seeing the alewives escape the pillory brought him some satisfaction, but the church thief tugged at him. Wikerus was an easygoing man, but he disliked situations with no resolution.

Instead of returning directly to the priory from Strassburg, Friar Wikerus had gone straight to the trial of the alewives. Now, as he led his weary little donkey through the streets and back toward the church, his mind turned from confessions of sinners to a bowl of porridge, a mug of warm wine, and the calming serenity of his prayers.

The familiar figure of Girard, the night watchman, slouched from an alley and into the main street, holding his pole-mounted lantern.

"Herr Girard," Wikerus called out. Girard waved in the dim light.

"Greetings, Friar. A bit late for you to be outside, is it not?"

"I am just returning from a journey to Strassburg. Girard, please take extra care to watch the alewives. Frau Appel is sleeping at Frau Efi's house until the murderer of the women in Les Tanneurs can be found, and I am worried for their safety."

Girard's face was concerned. "Aye, I saw them together, though I thought something else was going on. You know." He nudged Friar Wikerus in the ribs with an elbow and a wink.

"No, Girard, I can promise you that is not happening."

"Well, I feel safer knowing that Herr Widmer is under the lock, I'll tell you that much, Friar."

"And why is that?"

"'Cause I looked at the situation around his house with the sheriff, and there is no way anyone else could have done it. No footprints except his going in and out of the house. And many times when I passed in the night, I could hear them arguing something fierce, usually about money."

"You think that Herr Widmer killed his wife? And what about the other women who were murdered? Did he kill them too?"

"He could have done them too. I advised the sheriff to keep him locked up for more time, and he agreed."

Friar Wikerus furrowed his brow. "Very well. Please keep watch over the alewives at night, will you?"

"I will, Friar. You have my word on it!"

Finally, Wikerus saw the stone edifice of the narrow church looming before him. Next to the incomparably grand Cathedral of Notre Dame in Strassburg, the church was small, but it was beginning to feel like home. He led his little donkey to the stables, where a novice took over, and then trudged through the slippery courtyard toward the cloister for a change of clothes.

A movement caught his attention, and Wikerus spied a black-robed Dominican walking swiftly toward him in the shadows. It was Father Tacitus. Friar Wikerus took a deep breath and steeled himself for this confrontation. No doubt Tacitus was annoyed that the alewives still walked free. Wikerus tucked his hands into the sleeves of his robe and dipped his head.

"Greetings, Father Tacitus. You must have heard by now."

"Of course I've heard!" Tacitus snapped. "This is all your fault, you know."

Wikerus nodded solemnly, but his eyes twinkled. "But I also had the help of God, Tacitus. And God forgives."

"I doubt even God's forgiveness will extend in this case," Tacitus sneered. "This has all been a waste of time, and while you dither, the problems mount. You've been working on this little project long enough. It's time the prior assigned someone else to the task – someone with more wit and faith than you."

Wikerus blinked at Father Tacitus without comprehension. "The prior did not ask me to make contact with the alewives; I did it because I am commanded by my Franciscan order to go out and serve the community. I know in my heart that it is wrong to prevent those women from providing for themselves and their children."

"What are you talking about?" Tacitus demanded. "What do I care about those slatterns? I am talking about the altar gold."

"What?"

"The two gilt candlesticks were stolen while you were away, and they were taken directly from the locked storerooms. The last of the church's gold is gone."

Taking charge

In which Gritta remembers what happened to her hoe

T HE NEWS THAT THE Dominicans were now deprived of all their gold immediately rippled through the city of Colmar, from the aromatic streets of Les Tanneurs to the well-heeled burghers' quarter further up the hill. The alewives heard about it quickly enough as they were busy outside Appel's house, preparing to send an order of ale to Karl's inn.

"Well," Gritta mused as she watched Karl's two sons lever the large, slightly crooked ale barrels onto the scooped back of the two-wheeled cart. "It's not Friar Wikerus who stole the gold, for the candlesticks disappeared while he was away."

"But what about Herr Widmer? While he has been under the lock, there hasn't been a single murder. Could he really be the one who killed Hattie and Odile?" Efi asked.

"I have a hard time believing it, for Herr Widmer is as mild-mannered as his wife was a shrew. But I suppose a man can be pushed past his limits." She glanced at her house across the lane, where Jorges was setting out for his day of work in Lord Frider's fields. He whistled a jaunty tune as he walked, a simple meal of bread and some hard sausage wrapped in a scrap of cloth and tucked underneath his arm.

"And don't you return home with naught but a mouth full of foul breath and a head of wool like last time, you lout!" she yelled across the lane. "If you don't bring home enough coin for me to purchase a new hoe for my garden, I will force you to whittle one yourself!"

Jorges gave her a salute and then sauntered in the direction of the city gate.

"I must say, Gritta, Jorges is a good-natured man, even if he is usually sodden with the drink." Appel looked sideways at her friend. Gritta suppressed a smile, rearranging her face into its characteristic stern façade.

"Aye. It's a good job I'm here to ensure he is fed and watered."

"But if he ever strikes you again, Gritta, I shall paddle him with my largest soup ladle."

Gritta patted Appel on the arm. "I do believe you would, old friend."

Once the barrels were secured to the carts and hauled away, the three women scrubbed the pots for boiling the next batch of mash, scouring them with sand and plenty of fresh water. They threw the shutters open to cleanse the air in the house, swept the dropped bits of grain from the corners of the room to discourage vermin, and took an inventory of their stores of barley, honey, and herbs. Appel looked up from where she was sorting the dried myrtle leaves from the spikes of rosemary on a clean cloth.

"We must fetch water for the next brew, and since it must come from the priory now, it takes three times as long. And where has Gritta gone off to?"

"I'll find her." Efi wiped her brow, relieved to free herself from the banal task of removing the dead insects and dried twigs from the sack of heather buds. She found Gritta across the lane in the small garden next to her house, frowning down at her rows of wilting leeks, which had been carefully banked up with straw to keep them through the harsh frosts and snow of the winter. Her hands clutched at her bony hips.

"Well, Gritta, are you trying to escape the work as I am?" Efi laughed. "Are you still looking for your hoe? You are nearly rich enough to afford a new one!"

"I know where my hoe is," Gritta said quietly. "All this time I had forgotten, but I just remembered. I lent it to Frau Widmer last summer when she needed it to tend her cabbages. The poor woman was digging around her plants with her hands."

"Oh!" Efi put a hand over her mouth. "Before Hattie died?"

"Yes, before Hattie died."

"What are you going to do, Gritta?"

Gritta scowled across the street at the Widmer house.

"I am going to go bring it back." She pushed the sleeves of her dress to her elbows and marched through the garden, which was soggy with winter damp, and across Trench Lane with Efi at her heels.

Herr Widmer still languished in Sheriff Werner's cellar, insisting on his innocence, and the Widmer house had been empty for weeks now. Rotting leaves piled up against the doorposts, and its shuttered windows looked like sad, closed eyes. Even the storks who lived atop the roof had abandoned their shaggy nest since the heat from the hearth below no longer warmed the thatch.

"Gritta, I don't think it wise to go in the house," Efi fretted as Gritta walked resolutely to the front door and tried to push it open. "Frau Marguerite says she heard the spirit of Frau Widmer wailing from inside the house, calling out for the forgiveness of her sins. Perhaps we should first go to the church to pray her soul into a more peaceful state before we attempt to get inside her house." Efi was tugging on Gritta's sleeve and digging the heels of her leather boots into the muddy ground.

"It must be in the stable." Gritta ignored Efi and walked into the narrow alley behind the house. Here was where Frau Widmer had taken her last breath. Had she seen her attacker, or was it a surprise? Efi's head swiveled from side to side, eyes wide with terror as she walked behind her friend, clutching at Gritta's arm.

"Gritta, I am scared," she whispered.

"Then go back and help Appel. I need my hoe to till the earth before springtime, or else my garden will fail and my children will starve. It can't be called stealing if it's already mine."

"That's what Frau Widmer said to us before she was killed." Efi clutched Gritta's arm harder, and together they peeked inside the drafty little shelter of rotting wood that leaned against the back entrance of the house. Here they found a few worn tools, stacks of dry logs for the fire, a pile of hay that was once fresh but now moldering with dampness, and Odile's cabbage crock.

"Ha! So she also 'borrowed' Odile's crock!" Gritta crowed. "I always knew Frau Widmer was a thief and a liar."

"Oh, Gritta, we're going to hell for this," Efi said breathlessly. "I don't see a hoe in here. Let us go back and tell the sheriff. He can open the house for us. Or let us bring Girard. We need a man here to protect us!"

Gritta spun and faced Efi. The sight of the girl, her wimple slipping from her head and quaking with fear, softened the sharp response on Gritta's tongue. She took Efi's hand firmly.

"I will protect us."

Gritta stepped inside the stable, which was attached to the house, and pushed on the back door, testing its soundness. The doorframe had swollen from lack of use and the damp weather. Gritta put her shoulder against it, and the door scraped open. The two women peeked inside. The one-room house was dim and dusty. The interior had never been plastered, and the raw thatch gave the room an even darker appearance. A thick layer of dust and piles of mouse droppings covered the few pieces of furniture.

"Ah-ha! There it is! I see my hoe next to the hearth. The wench had no intention of giving it back to me." Gritta stepped inside, with Efi following gingerly, still clutching her hand. There was a great shuffling and fluttering in the rafters, and Efi screamed, leaping backward and tugging Gritta toward the door, but the older woman stood firm, hauling Efi into the center of the room.

"It is only an owl, you silly girl. See, there is a small portal near the roof that is open, and that is how it enters and leaves. There are enough rats in this house that the owl probably doesn't even have to go out at night to hunt if it's feeling lazy." She snatched the hoe from where it leaned against the hearth, dislodging a stone from the blackened chimney, which fell to the floor with a loud crack.

Efi, her nerves jumping, yelped in surprise and jumped back toward the room's darkest corner, stumbling over a bench with an unearthly clatter. She landed with her backside in a large basket of wool.

"Ow!"

Gritta hurried over to help her to her feet. "Well, I had hoped to come in and quietly get my tool back. Now, if there are ghosts or demons in this house, you have woken them all, Efi. Honestly, you are as nervous as a black cat in a church nave!"

"There's something underneath this wool, and it's sharp." Efi rubbed her back and gasped when she looked at her hand in the dim light. Her palms were dark red with bloodstains. "Oh, it hurts. And I've torn my cotte, too."

Gritta heaved Efi to her feet, and together they dragged the basket, which was suspiciously heavy, into the center of the room, where the light seeped through the gaps in the shutters. In the golden shafts of the early morning sun, something warm and rich gleamed up at them from inside the basket. Gritta reached underneath the wool and gently lifted a large object: a wooden crucifix with gold-plated tips had a red bloodstain where it had ripped Efi's dress and scratched her back. For a moment, the two women stared at it. Gritta knelt and reached out a trembling hand to the basket, brushing a gilt candlestick with her fingertips.

"Just need to make sure I am not imagining things," she laughed nervously.

"Gritta, it's the altar gold. The stolen gold from the church!"

Gritta nodded her head dumbly.

"So it was the Widmers who were stealing it!"

"No." Gritta picked up a candlestick and held it to the light. "This candlestick was in the church after Frau Widmer was found dead. You and I saw them both at Matins. The candlesticks were the last items stolen from the church, and they were taken only a few days ago. Herr Widmer is locked in a cellar, so it isn't him. Whoever took these knows this house is empty and has access to it."

"Indeed," a voice spoke behind them. "I truly did not expect cunning from a couple of slovenly alewenches. I am impressed."

The women jumped up and Gritta pushed Efi behind her. A man's figure was silhouetted in the dim, dusty light. Efi gasped, and Gritta sighed heavily.

"Of course. We should have known it would be you."

The missing women

In which Friar Wikerus is determined to save two lives

APPEL THREW UP HER hands and snarled a few choice epithets at her two missing friends. She had waited for the entire morning, and neither Efi nor Gritta had returned. She had sent out one of Gritta's sons – she had no idea which one – to search Efi's house, the market, the public privy, and the church. Not only did the little whelp return without his mother, but he demanded a copper from Appel for his troubles. Appel gave him a withered onion and told him to be grateful he didn't receive a cuff across the ear instead.

But the boy's visit to the church had brought Friar Wikerus, his face etched with concern for the two missing women.

"I am sure they just became distracted. Efi is very empty-headed, as you know, Friar Wikerus," Appel said, shaking her head. "The girl needs constant supervision or else she is prone to idleness."

"But Gritta is not empty-headed or idle," Friar Wikerus said, "and that is why I wonder at their whereabouts, for Gritta would not leave work undone and her children unfed for the noon meal. And if she were here, she would be complaining about Efi's absence. No, my dear woman, I think that they are together."

The comment drove a stake of fear through Appel's breast. He spoke the truth about her friend. Gritta might be ill-tempered, but she was a responsible woman.

"Where is Jorges, Frau Appel?"

"Working in Lord Frider's fields on this day and the next," Appel said, her eyes scanning the crowds of people who clogged the street near the market. "They are breaking the soil for next year's turnips."

"I see. Let us fetch the sheriff first and leave Jorges to his work, for I know that the family needs the money." He turned sharply to Appel. "Unless it is his compulsory service?"

"No, Friar. Indeed, you haven't lived in Colmar very long. We are a free city, and no one owes labor to a lord. Jorges receives a wage for his work. A very small wage, but enough to buy some grain, provided he doesn't spend his coppers at the weinstube on his way home from the fields."

"I see. I shall find the sheriff at all haste. I have an ill feeling about this. Do you think you can find Girard, the night watchman? He will be of great assistance in our search, for he knows all the places that one might be able to hide a—" Friar Wikerus stopped abruptly, his eyes darting at Appel.

"Hide a body." Appel finished his sentence for him. Friar Wikerus answered with a serious, blue-eyed stare, and Appel felt the tears spring to her eyes. "Saints preserve us, Friar Wikerus!"

"Pray, Frau Appel," Friar Wikerus said as he grasped the long hem of his robe. "Pray harder than you have ever prayed before." He hitched his robe around his shins and ran down the street and through the crowded market toward the weinstube. Before him, the shoppers and merchants parted in waves to let him pass as they stared after him.

Appel took a moment to wipe her eyes and compose herself, then set out to find Girard.

The sheriff was not at the winemaker's guild nor in the weinstube, and thank the lord Jesu Christi for that, for how would Friar Wikerus manage a drunken sheriff and a grieving husband if Efi and Gritta were indeed murdered?

After a rousing trot around the streets, in which he elicited many shouts of surprise and jest from the passersby, Wikerus discovered the sheriff at the stables, lecturing the young farrier on the best way to shoe a horse. The farrier, whose trade was in shoeing horses day in and day out, listened politely, but his face flooded with relief when the panting and puffing friar gasped out the news about the two missing women.

"This is distressing information, indeed, Friar," Sheriff Werner said, and after dispensing a few more words of instruction to the farrier, he followed Friar Wikerus back to Les Tanneurs. "Phew, it always stuns me when I enter this quarter," he said with a laugh. "It makes me wonder why a murderer would not try to find victims in a more pleasant-smelling part of city. Next to him, Friar Wikerus's face was stony.

They found Appel where Friar Wikerus had left her, wringing her hands and pacing in her dooryard amongst the chickens. Two other tanners' wives sat on the bench outside Appel's door – one knitting furiously and another sorting a basket of onions. At their feet, three young children played with Appel's striped ginger cat, who purred and stretched luxuriously under their tiny hands. One of the children was Wina, Gritta's youngest. Friar Wikerus glanced at Gritta's house across the lane. Her twin boys were standing in the doorway, looking solemnly at the frantic activity.

Friar Wikerus hopped across the trench and smiled at the twins, who backed inside the house. "Hello, Anstett. Hello Mattheus. Is your sister at home?"

"No, but Lonel's here," Anstett said. "Rosmunda is out courtin' with the potter's son."

Friar Wikerus stored that information away for later. He might have to find the young man and Rosmunda to collect confessions in the coming days. "Well, I shall speak with Lonel, then."

He stepped inside the house and found Gritta's middle-born son sitting on the packed dirt in front of the hearth, staring sightlessly into the glowing coals.

"Lonel, you are aware that your mother and young widow Efi are missing?"

The boy closed his eyes at Friar Wikerus's words but did not move. Friar Wikerus watched him for a moment, thinking.

"Lonel, is there something you need to tell me?"

Slowly, Lonel turned to look at the holy man. His eye still displayed a dark shadow where he had been struck only days earlier after his escapades in Herr Volker's sheep pen.

"I know who has been stealing your altar gold, Friar Wikerus. And I think he also killed my mother."

Friar Wikerus dashed from Gritta's dim house into the late morning sun, his head swiveling as he searched the courtyard for Sheriff Werner. The man was nowhere to be found, but Appel was still outside her house, pacing and scolding Gritta's children. Wikerus hurried to her.

"Appel, where is the sheriff? I must find him at once!"

"H-he's—" Appel stifled a sob "—he's setting the men to work raking the grand canal in case Gritta and Efi..." but she couldn't finish her sentence. The thought of her two dearest friends floating lifeless in the canal was too much.

Friar Wikerus grasped her shoulders. "Appel, listen to me. I know who killed the other women in Les Tanneurs. Take Gritta's children, go into her house, bar the door, and do not open it for anyone except the sheriff or myself." He had picked up little Wina in one arm and was leading Appel by the hand across the lane. He waited until he heard Appel slide the bar down over the door to Gritta's house before he marched back to Appel's house to scatter the gaggle of goodwives who stood in the lane and waited with vicious anticipation. After he had shouted them back into their homes, he snatched up the alewives' long, wooden mash paddle, steeled his nerves, and marched down Trench Lane.

It was dark and dusty inside Frau Widmer's empty house. Friar Wikerus, whose shorn head was damp with a sheen of sweat, remembered a few details from his only visit to Frau Widmer, and they remained the same: a massive, sooty stone hearth, two benches on either side of a trestle table, and baskets of items that Frau Widmer had acquired. She had insisted that the contents of the baskets were all legally gained, but he knew from Herr Widmer's confessions that his wife had been stealing small items from her neighbors for years and then accusing them of stealing from her in turn.

A quick look around the room told him that this house had been recently occupied. He could see the marks of disturbed dust and earth where a scuffle had taken place, and a hoe lay in the middle of the room on the floor. Wikerus reached down slowly and picked the hoe up, holding it in surprisingly steady hands. The shaft of the tool felt reassuring and familiar. For a moment, Wikerus was back in a field again, facing down the bandits that had burned his father's farm and stolen his mother and sister.

Wikerus shook his head until the memories vanished. Now was not the time to dwell on the past. If he could prevent two more women from ravage and death, his soul might find some ease. Shuffling further into the room in a crouch, he was aware that he must look strange. Friars were supposed to be gentle and wise, chaste and temperate. Wikerus knew that God commanded him not to do violence, and he also knew at this moment that he did not care. If it meant his reassignment to yet another priory, so be it. He took another shuffling step forward, the hoe raised high, and a voice spoke into the dark.

"Not another move, Friar, or my knife plunges into her throat."

Criminal confession

In which Lonel becomes crucial to the story

"TELL ME AGAIN, LONEL," Appel demanded. "Tell me how you came by your black eye?"

"Sometimes Girard the night watchman would let me watch the streets in the night," Lonel said sullenly. "I wore his leather cap and carried the pole lantern. Sometimes the other lads would do it as well. We would hammer on the doors and scold people who were tupping loudly." He chuckled. "Scared them half to death, we did, while they were in the act."

"Why is your eye blackened? Your mother said it is because you were riding Herr Vogel's sheep."

"Ah, well I was, and that is why my eye was blackened the first time. Herr Vogel is half-blind, and he thought I was having a romp with his daughter, Marion. As if I would do such a thing." Lonel snorted. "Her body has an odor of cheese about it."

"And why was your eye blackened a second time?"

"One night, Girard asked me to take the night watch, but I didn't wish it. I was readying myself to meet Marie, the miller's daughter, for a bit of a cuddle, but Girard insisted I take the lantern and do his rounds for him. Lately, he had started getting belligerent about it, swaggering about and acting like the other lads and I were his serfs and he a liege lord. I said no, and he struck me on my other eye, then said if I told anyone the real reason why I was injured, he'd tell my ma and the prior that I had been meeting Marie in the nights. Girard knows a lot of things about a lot of people." Lonel looked directly at Appel now, and she squirmed underneath his bruised gaze. "A lot of things. He saves what he knows about people so he can use it to threaten them later."

Appel jumped to her feet. The day had mostly passed, and the sun was making its late afternoon transit toward the horizon. The younger children were all inside the house – Wina playing with a ball of string, Egilhard drawing pictures in the packed earthen floor with a sharpened stick, and the twins, Anstett and Mattheus, were methodically disassembling an oakwood chair and whittling one of the legs into something that looked like a phallus in full, erect splendor. Appel chanced a look out the shutters on the window. Trench Lane was empty, no doubt because of the warnings of Friar Wikerus. But where was the good friar now? He had been gone since the morning, and her stomach flipped a few times with dread. She turned back to Lonel who was sniffling now, still sitting in front of the fire where she had found him.

"Did Girard give you instruction to be near a specific place when you took his watch?"

"Not usually, although there were a few times when he said he had already finished Les Tanneurs and I didn't need to do the rounds there. I was happy enough because my voice would be recognized so close to home anyways. Frau Appel, do you think he killed my ma?"

Appel felt that lurch of fear in her breast once again. She paced the room, her arms folded. "Well, young man, we must determine that ourselves. What do we know?"

Lonel stared up at her, bewildered for a moment. "We know that Girard is probably the person who stole the altar gold," he said slowly.

"Indeed. He had you dress in his clothes and take on his duties so he could claim he had been nowhere near the church, but the thefts all happened at night."

"Aye, and he had a black robe like a Dominican. If he wore it, he wouldn't be noticed roaming the streets in the dark and would not appear suspicious to one of the brothers if seen from afar."

Appel looked up in alarm. "He had the robe of a Blackfriar?"

"Not exactly, it was just a long, black wool cloak, but from a distance, it was difficult to tell that it wasn't the garb of a friar."

"The wearing of black should be outlawed!" Appel hissed. "It is the Devil's color."

"And the dead women? What about them, Frau Appel?"

"They must have caught him somehow." She was quiet for a moment, walking and thinking. "Of course! Hattie Jungerwald was out late at night because she had been screaming at

Frau Widmer. According to your ma, Girard intervened and broke up their argument, but then Hattie was still livid and ranting afterward, yelling loudly enough to wake the entire square. Girard probably knew he was safe because many curious neighbors saw him separate the two women and then continue out of Les Tanneurs on his rounds. But if Hattie remained outside after everyone had lost interest, she might have encountered him as he attempted to move the stolen gold from one place to another."

"I didn't do the watch the night Hattie died," Lonel offered. "And neither did the other lads."

"So Hattie could have seen Girard and addressed him by name."

"And Odile?"

"This murder is puzzling indeed. Odile was the wife of the basket weaver, a mother, and a pious woman. There was no reason why she would be out late at night," Appel mused. She saw Lonel flush slightly.

"Not so pious, Frau Appel. Marie told me she sometimes spied Frau Odile sneaking out of the house once all were asleep, creeping to the stables of Enguerrand, the farrier, in the night."

"So, she could have been out visiting her lover and come across Girard. Where were you that night when Odile was murdered?"

"I was hammering on doors near the smithy."

Appel nodded. "And that was the night that the gold cross was stolen from the church nave. Girard was once again transferring his stolen goods from the church, but if Odile were out extremely late, he would have been startled to find her, and she might have been equally alarmed to see him dressed as a Dominican friar."

"I doubt she had much time for distress," Lonel said miserably. "Girard is a strong man. He could have drowned Odile and broken her neck before she even had a chance to scream."

Appel swallowed heavily, pushing the mental image of her fair neighbor and a goodwife of Les Tanneurs being submerged and strangled at the same time.

"And then there is Frau Widmer. She was murdered right outside her own door."

"Girard was bragging that he had convinced the sheriff to keep Herr Widmer locked in the storeroom as a suspect." Lonel stood now, growing animated. "At the time, he said it was because Herr Widmer was clearly ready to be rid of his shrew wife, but now I think that the blame would look to be on the husband, not on himself."

"Aye, but why on earth would Girard be in the alley behind the Widmer house in the first place?"

They both fell silent in their thoughts until only the crackling hearth made any sound in the room. Rosmunda was out at the privy, and Wina had curled up to sleep on Egilhard's chest. Noe would not be back until his duties with the cooper were finished for the day. In a corner, Anstett and Mattheus had fallen asleep on the basket of dyed wool that Gritta and Efi had prepared only days earlier.

"Poor Gritta," Appel whispered. "She didn't even have time to spin this beautiful wool. She dyed it because Frau Widmer kept accusing her of stealing it."

"Frau Widmer accused everyone of stealing from her."

"She said she had come into money recently..." Appel frowned.

"Perhaps," Lonel mused. "But Frau Widmer took things from everyone. Once, when I was in Eguisheim with my papi, we saw her selling Cateline Gastwirt's red and yellow hair ribbon in the market there."

"But she was noisy – always complaining, always yelling, and making accusations against people. She must have known what Girard was up to and demanded he pay her to keep quiet. He would have to do it or else kill her."

"I was doing the watch for Girard that night," Lonel said, tears running down his face now. "But I was near the church, I swear it, Frau Appel! I didn't have nothing to do with Frau Widmer's death."

"I believe you, boy, but now is no time for tears. We must find out where Girard is because that is where we will find your mother, Efi, and I suspect, Friar Wikerus as well."

Appel walked to the door and pulled it open.

"Frau Appel, Friar Wikerus told you not to open the door," Lonel reminded her.

"Bar it behind me, young man, and mind your brothers and sister. I am going to find my friends."

Throats

In which three throats are in mortal danger

WITH EACH MOMENT THAT the light in the already dim, abandoned home of the Widmers grew fainter, so grew Girard the night watchman's panic. He had become overconfident. After all, it wasn't hard to convince the sheriff and the nosy man of the church that the deaths of Frau Odile and that haggard old gossip, Hattie Jungerwald, were accidental. Still, everyone was on alert after Frau Widmer. He snorted and shook his head. It was unsurprising that, even in death, Frau Widmer still managed to draw attention to herself and torment him from beyond her grave.

"Three bodies," he muttered aloud. "How will I move this many? The women are easy enough, but that friar..." He shot a baleful look at the two women. "Ale-swilling, tannery-stinking whores, the lot of you!" he snarled. From where she sat, tied to a chair and gagged with a stocking, the widow Efi whimpered. In the gloom of the room, he could see the black trickle of dried blood where he had managed to puncture the delicate skin of her white throat. That busybody friar did not take Girard seriously when he threatened to sever Efi's pretty blonde head from her shoulders. All it took was the first sight of blood, and Friar Wikerus had dropped his weapon.

He shot a nervous glance in the direction of the friar, who lay facedown and motionless on the hard-packed earthen floor of the house, a puddle of blood still trickling from where Girard had struck him right on the top of his tonsure. Girard knew that his soul was already bound for hell. After all, he had stolen relics from the church. Killing a holy man would not make him any more damned than he already was.

A wicked smile spread across Girard's face. "Of course! It is only fitting that I should remove your corpses from this house with an ale cart." He winced, his confidence immediately broken as the sound of conversation from the nearby street penetrated the room. The Widmer house was directly on the square, and the heavily trafficked Trench Lane was constantly busy with market-goers, children playing, tanners meeting with clients, and goodwives laughing with each other outside their homes. Until the inhabitants of Les Tanneurs settled into their homes for the evening meal and last chores before the light was gone, Girard was trapped in this house with not two but three victims, all needing attention.

Wikerus was easy enough, unconscious as he was. Efi wouldn't be too difficult – just a quick slash across the two largest veins of the throat, the way his father had taught him when he was the under-butcher in Eguisheim. But Frau Gritta was a problem.

The best he could do was tie Gritta to one of the supporting posts that held up the roof of the house with a few pieces of clothing he'd found in a chest. Despite his threats, Gritta had yelled and screamed, and in his desperation to shut her up, he had stuffed a ball of yarn into her mouth. Even with a mouth full of wool, she could still make a lot of noise, and she did.

Girard sighed heavily. All he had wanted was a little extra coin. Being a night watchman was a fine enough occupation, but he had no wife and children, and neither could he afford to marry unless he somehow managed to amass enough silver. He could move from his free city of Colmar to a different town or village which owed its allegiance to a lord and perhaps obtain the lord's protection in exchange for back-breaking labor and high taxes, but Girard was loyal to Colmar. For years he had patrolled her streets in the darkness. Behind the shutters of the houses, he could hear the voices of her people – the arguments, the banal discussions, the moans of pleasure, and the snores of exhaustion. His wanderings took him past the same places again and again, and he watched her buildings grow along with the city's prosperity. He observed the changing of the seasons as the streets became rutted in the spring and dried out in the summer, and as the level of the water in the canals and streams rose and fell according to the whims of the mountain brooks.

He hadn't meant to hurt anyone, but the alleys and lanes of his city were not as empty as he had always assumed. First, Hattie Jungerwald had caught him with the gold chain of an incense censor dripping from his sack as he darted from the church to the special place where he hid his treasures – a loose stone in the city wall. Only a short time earlier, he had forcibly separated her from an argument in the street with Frau Widmer and assumed the old busybody was abed. When she loudly declared that she would have him dragged to the prior, he didn't think twice about putting his hands around her scrawny throat.

The second time, Frau Widmer found him as he crept over a stile near the Church of the Dominicans, and she quickly determined that he was up to some sort of mischief. But he had some leverage over her, for, after the murder, he had seen Frau Widmer remove the white and brown chemise from Hattie Jungerwald's still-cooling body and stuff it into her sack before slinking off to her own home. Presumably, Frau Widmer had entered the old widow's house to give her a second round of tongue-lashing but found her dead instead. It was easy for Girard to use this information to shut Frau Widmer up, and that is when he came up with his idea to use her house to hide his stolen goods.

Being a poor man, he lived in a shared lodging with seven other bachelors and two impoverished families. At night, they all snored together in the straw, as Girard set out for his work with the lantern and his cudgel, and in the morning, the widow who owned the place gave them some thin pottage of barley and turnips before she turned them out for the day. By the time Girard returned home from his nighttime duties, the straw was flat and cold, and the pottage nearly gone. If only he had a little more silver in his pocket, he could afford to take a house and a wife. And one night, as he made his rounds near the church of the Dominicans, and saw how loosely they guarded their treasures, the solution to his problems became clear.

Hiding stolen church gold in his rented house was out of the question. But the children playing near the city wall would notice his hiding place behind the loose stone eventually, and Girard's heart thundered and his nerves twitched all day as he wondered when he would be discovered. Hiding the goods with Frau Widmer was the best solution, for if they were found, she would be implicated as the thief. All he needed to do was give her a silver button or buckle every now and again to keep her quiet.

And then there was Frau Odile. He closed his eyes as he recalled how her arms thrashed and then stilled as he held her head under the water of the canal. Why was she even out that night? If only she had remained inside, he wouldn't have had to do it. Frau Odile was kind, gentle, and fair to look upon, too. He hadn't wanted to kill anyone, least of all her, but she caught him in the act as he removed a relic from the church's altar. She was a fast runner, and it took him a while to catch her as she fled, but catch her he did, and now he wished he hadn't.

Girard didn't consider himself an evil man or even a violent man. All of his actions were justified in his mind. Why shouldn't he have an opportunity for a better life? If God was in heaven, why did he need so much earthly gold?

Abruptly, Girard stopped his nervous pacing and turned toward Efi. "'Tis a shame, for you are young and fair. But I can't have you crying out, and I cannot wait in here any longer, or someone will notice my absence. I'll make this quick and as painless as possible, young woman." He thumbed the blade of his dagger and then nodded his head to give himself courage. Yes, it must be done. This was for the good of his future. "Best to do this now."

Girard advanced on Efi, whose tears were running down her cheeks and soaking the wool stocking he had tied around her mouth. "You're going first so as you don't suffer. I want her to go last because she's a vile wench who deserves to watch." He jerked his chin at Gritta, who roared through her ball of saliva-soaked yarn. On the floor, Friar Wikerus stirred and moaned weakly against his thick gag.

Girard looked at the holy man with alarm. Perhaps it would be better to do the friar first, since he was still unable to move. But Efi's whimpers and Gritta's muffled curses jarred his nerves. He felt his irritation rising.

"Just do it, old boy," he told himself. "This has gone on for long enough."

Positioning himself behind Efi, Girard put the knife to her throat, grasping her chin with one hand. He tried to shush her, but she bucked and turned her head violently from side to side.

"Oh, hold still, why don't you!" he whispered harshly. He pushed her chair until she fell backward and slammed her head against the dirt floor, and for a moment she was stunned and silent. Then he pounced upon her, wrapping his thick fingers around her throat. The flesh of her throat was younger and plumper than Hattie Jungerwald's, and he felt a sob rise from his stomach. He didn't want to murder any more people. Perhaps there was a way that he could extract himself from this whole mess without causing any more death.

That was the last thought that fluttered through his mind before the blow struck the back of his head, and he fell senseless to the floor.

A murderer. A thief.

In which Appel breaks her mash paddle

As SOON AS HER hands were untied, Gritta pulled the ball of yarn from her mouth and spat the taste of ripe sheep and greasy lanolin to the floor. She squinted up at her rescuer, then sighed, long and heavy.

"Well, that took you long enough."

Appel planted her hands on her hips, a posture of indignation as she stood over her friend. "Apologies if I inconvenienced you, my dear," she said in a saccharine voice. "I would have come here sooner, but I did not realize it would take me such a long time to force a confession from your son, Lonel, first." She strode to the window and threw the shutters open. The blueish light of an overcast evening seeped inside but did little else to relieve the gloom of the abandoned house.

Efi, recently freed from her own bonds, was angrily brushing dust and bits of straw from her frock.

"Ripped in two places now," she snarled as she fingered her tattered cotte. "And this fine linen was a gift from my Harald, too. He said it matched my eyes."

"That linen is red, Efi. It only matches your eyes when you're weeping or drinking," Gritta snapped.

"Well, that's just lovely. No thanks from either of you ungrateful wenches, and after I saved you from the knife!" Appel declared. "And look, I broke my best mash paddle when I struck Girard over the head with it!" She picked up the two halves of her destroyed weapon and stared at them, one in each hand, despondently.

They heard a moan as Girard stirred from where he had fallen on the floor. In an instant, Efi snatched up Gritta's hoe and walloped Girard over the head with it. He fell still and silent.

"Not my hoe, you daft girl!" Gritta shrieked. "Not after all the trouble I went through to get it back!"

"For the love of Jesu, will the three of you please stop arguing," Friar Wikerus groaned as he slowly rose to his feet, clutching the top of his shorn head. "Be pleased that you all live! For truth, your complaining can be heard all the way from here to Hades and everywhere in between."

"Friar Wikerus!" the three women all said in unison.

Wikerus winced at the noise of their voices. "Well," he said sheepishly, rubbing the back of his bruised skull. "I don't suppose I'll ever become a knight after word of this comes out."

Appel helped him to a bench while Gritta and Efi set about tying Girard's hands with his own leather girdle. Then they dragged the wool basket of altar gold under the window so they could examine the contents in the dying light.

"Someone ought to fetch the prior," Wikerus said weakly, still clutching his head.

"How about the sheriff?" Appel said in a grim voice. "Here comes the big oaf now."

Sheriff Werner sauntered through the square of Les Tanneurs with two of his lackeys in tow and Lonel following behind at a distance.

"Lonel, I told you to remain at home with the young'uns, you worthless child!" Gritta yelled, stabbing an accusing finger at her son. "No better than his father, this one," she grumbled. But Lonel's face brightened, and a vast grin showed off his mouth full of crooked teeth.

"Ma!" he yelled as he loped toward the open window of the house. "I was acting on the orders of Frau Appel, Ma. She told me to find the sheriff and come straight to the Widmer house."

"Lies," Appel said, crossing her arms over her chest.

Lonel peeked inside the house and his eyes widened at the sight of a basket of gold next to the unconscious form of Girard. "What have you got here, Ma?"

As Appel turned to Sheriff Werner, Efi and Gritta both moved to stand behind her.

"What I have here is a murderer and a thief."

Industrious, clever, and loyal

In which Friar Wikerus defends his new friends

F RIAR WIKERUS LOOKED AT the floor, hoping his face displayed the appropriate amount of penitence as Father Konrad paced in front of him.

"Imagine my shock and surprise when Sheriff Werner told me that you, of all people, were trussed up like a goose inside the Widmer house and about to lose your life along with three slovenly alewives! A man of God should know better!"

"They are not slovenly," Friar Wikerus said. "They are industrious, clever, and loyal. Show me a guildsman in this city who runs his business as well as they."

The prior waved his arms in the air. "They are not supposed to be running a business! The widows should be married, and Frau Gritta has twelve children to care for!"

"Only eight at home," Wikerus muttered, and the prior shot him a look of warning.

"She cannot possibly have the time to brew and sell more ale than her ravenous husband can consume. But never mind, never mind. It is all settled now." Father Konrad waved his hand dismissively, and Wikerus narrowed his eyes.

"How has it been settled, my lord? Unless you mean that Girard is apprehended – by the three of them – and most of the gold has been returned to the church. That which he didn't sell already, of course. Had I been able to ascertain the identity of the thief earlier, perhaps more gold would have been saved, but instead, I spent too much time doubting the wisdom of three women who know when something is not right in their own city."

"Brother Wikerus, see here. I know you are fond of these women, but their behavior has been abominable, and it implicated you, involving you in a crime that was a matter for the laypeople and not the church. They distracted you from your duties by making you focus on the murders of impoverished women in Les Tanneurs instead of keeping your eyes and heart dedicated to matters of the church, namely, the theft of holy items."

Friar Wikerus, usually a calm man, felt his ire rising. "Prior, did you not instruct me to determine who was stealing the altar gold from the church?"

"Indeed, and you did admirably."

"No, my lord, I did not do admirably. I did not solve that crime; the alewives did. And what is more, those murders were directly tied to the thefts in the church. The dead women of Les Tanneurs were killed because they had all caught the thief at his work. One led to another."

"Yes, the loss of life is regrettable, especially after so many died in the pestilence—"

"But it's less regrettable because, after all, they were just widows and poor tanners' wives, is it not true, Father?" Friar Wikerus's voice was iron and his eyes blue ice. "If Lord Frider's wife were to be found strangled, drowned, or stabbed through the heart, every house in the city would have been turned inside out until the murderer had been flushed from his hiding place, would you not agree?"

"I have not told the alewives they cannot brew, Brother Wikerus, for that would be a terrible affliction upon them. Frau Gritta may brew for her family, and if she has surplus ale, she may sell it to her neighbors for a small profit. However, the widows, Frau Appel and Frau Efi, may not brew, and I have counseled them to find husbands as quickly as possible so they may avoid sin."

"You would take away the prosperity their hard work has earned them?" Now Wikerus's temper was burning.

"Do not become rebellious with me, Brother Wikerus." The prior shook a finger. "I will send you back to the Franciscans in Breisach if I must. I only accepted you here in this city because of my long-standing friendship with Father Guillaume, and you are here at my pleasure. Neither he nor you will tell me why you were sent away, and I haven't asked questions, but I must insist now that you tell me what happened in Breisach!"

For a moment, there was a deep, heavy silence. Friar Wikerus looked down at the scuffed toes of his suede boots and tucked his hands into the sleeves of his robes.

"It is true that I committed a sin at Breisach, my lord, but God and my own brothers at the priory have absolved me."

"And you have sinned here, haven't you, Brother Wikerus?"

When Friar Wikerus didn't answer, Father Konrad picked up a scrap of parchment on his table and moved it back and forth in front of his eyes until he could read the scrawled words properly. "According to the friars who manage the priory's larder, there is no way to explain the absence of seven bags of barley, as well as two pecks of gruit herbs from the brewing cabinet. I suppose you don't know anything about these missing items?"

"I only wanted to help them succeed," Friar Wikerus whispered.

The prior's stern face softened. He could press the young fellow for a more satisfactory answer, but why should he? Friar Wikerus had a way with the residents of Les Tanneurs, and for that the prior was grateful, though he would never admit it aloud. None of the other brothers could stomach the place because of the smell and the manners of its inhabitants, but Wikerus didn't seem to mind. It wasn't a serious bother to keep him around. In fact, it would be more of a chore to explain to Father Guillaume why Wikerus was being sent back. Questions would arise, and the prior of Colmar did not feel like discussing the theft of so much church gold on his watch.

Friar Wikerus knew that the Franciscans in Breisach would probably not take him back. He chose to push thoughts of his troublesome past away. This situation did not call for his temper; it called for his cunning. He took a deep breath and relaxed his tense shoulders, then hung his head in the most humble posture he could muster.

"Forgive me, my lord. I have been rebellious. I will spend the next three evenings in prayer to confess my sins of pride and arrogance before God and seek peace and serenity."

The prior nodded, his face triumphant. "There now, Brother. You are still young and still learning the ways of life. In truth, I am proud of how doggedly you pursued the problem of the stolen altar gold, and I have written to the prior in Breisach and told him so. Your talent and intellect are worthy of note."

"I thank you, my lord." Wikerus took the prior's hand and kissed it, then turned to leave but stopped.

"My lord, I wonder if we might find a compromise to the problem of these alewives. I think there might be a solution that helps everyone."

The prior sighed when he realized it was too much to assume that the stubborn friar would give up without more of a fight. "Go on," he said. "I am listening."

Friar Wikerus knew precisely where to find the alewives, and he headed directly for Appel's house at the far upwind portion of the canal, where the air and the water were the freshest. He smiled as he approached. Even from a distance he could hear Gritta scolding one of her children and Appel and Efi as they hurled good-natured insults at one another. The funk of boiling barley and herbs wafted on the breeze, and he noted that it pushed away the smell of the tanneries, making this part of the city almost pleasant. For a moment, he stood outside the door, unnoticed, wondering how he would break the news to them, then he tapped on the doorpost and walked in.

Gritta was wagging a finger at her daughter, Rosmunda, who held her squirming little sister, Wina, under an arm.

"And did I not tell you to keep your baby sister from swallowing the cold pieces of wood from the fire? If you had swept the house as I had asked, this never would have happened!"

Wina looked up and grinned. Her teeth, tongue, lips, and cheeks were all black with soot, and Friar Wikerus let out a laugh in spite of himself.

"Oh, leave her here then, and go prepare the pottage!" Gritta snapped, sending Rosmunda rushing out the door past him.

"Greetings, alewives. How goes the brew today?"

"Poorly, Friar." Appel straightened her back from where she labored over a steaming cauldron and massaged her neck. "This dimwit used the wrong herbs, and now this batch will be fit for naught but the pigs." She jerked a thumb at Efi, who had crossed her arms and sulked over the steaming pile of spent grain.

"Ain't my fault if yarrow and tansy look exactly the same," she muttered.

"They are different colors, Efi! Tansy is yellow and yarrow is white, and how hard is it to tell the difference between those? Your head is full of uncombed wool!"

"My dear goodwives, may I command your attention for a few moments?" Friar Wikerus sat on the bench next to Gritta, but not too close, lest she cuff him across the head after what he had to tell them.

Appel banked the fire down to keep the brew at a simmer, then gave him her full attention. Wikerus cleared his throat nervously.

"I've been talking with the prior, who has been talking with the sheriff and the city council. They are unhappy that the three of you are brewing together, especially you, Frau Appel, and you, Frau Efi. Of course, it is the wish of the council and the church that you both seek to find husbands so that you may keep from sin. Frau Gritta, you may brew and continue to sell what excess you have in order to support your family."

For a moment, the women were silent. Efi's eyes filled with tears. "But, Friar Wikerus, these women are my family," she sniffed. "I do not wish to replace my Harald so quickly and join another man's bed."

"And why should she?" Appel crossed her arms. "No one told me to remarry after my Giles died. I am not as young as Efi, and I suppose the status of my cunny was not interesting to the men of the council, was it?"

Efi and Gritta looked at Appel in shock, for she, being the most pious, would never utter such rebellion or profanity. And yet, she had.

"The prior and the city council feel that you three should not be doing this kind of work without a man's oversight. As the people are to be governed by God, so are women to be governed by their husbands." He ducked just as Gritta's hand reached out to slap his tonsured head.

"Put us all back into poverty, will you?! After what we did to help you catch the thief of your missing gold, did we get a word of thanks?!" She was on her feet now, shouting, and Friar Wikerus held up his hands in defense.

"Now wait, Gritta, just let me explain—"

"Explain nothing to me! We thought you were different, but you are not. You are the same as the rest of the men in this city."

"But wait until you hear what I have to say—"

"I will hear no more from you! If the so-called council wants us to stop brewing, then they can send Sheriff Werner here to arrest me and lock me in the storeroom with Girard!"

"But—"

Appel linked her arm to Efi's, and the two women grabbed Gritta, making a chain of resistance.

"I think you should go, Friar Wikerus," Efi said coldly, and Wikerus grinned. He crossed his arms and leaned back on the bench.

"I have told the prior and the council that I will do it. I will be the man who oversees your work." The women's outraged expressions were turning to blank stares.

"What?" Gritta asked. "We just told you we don't need no man."

"But you do, and please wait before you attempt to strike me again!" He jumped up and darted across the room as Gritta's hand shot out again. "You may run things as you wish – as you always have. I am only here to check in and assure the prior that you are not sinning. I will be the same as Jorges when he was your...what did you call him? Your 'hood.'"

"Jorges stole all our hard-earned coin," Appel said, narrowing her eyes.

"You may collect the coin yourselves."

"And you'll not interfere?"

"No. I offered myself as an alternative because I think that you three have a talent for this, that you have supported and protected each other in a time of need, and, as you said, you did not receive acknowledgment for the work that you did to catch Girard. It is not fair that, after all you have done, you should then be told to give up your livelihood."

The three alewives glanced at each other. Gritta put her hands on her hips.

"If you start to interfere, this arrangement is forfeit, and we will not allow you inside the door."

"Agreed. I haven't the time to interfere anyway, for I have duties in the community and the church."

"And no spyin' and speaking to that pompous prior about us," Appel sniffed.

"No spying. Agreed."

"And you will supply us with honey cakes if we ask it," Efi declared, and the other two women turned to stare at her.

"What are you talking about, you daft girl!" Gritta roared.

"Well, while you were both demanding things from the Friar, I thought I would too."

The friar's face broke into his characteristic, luminous smile, and he sat on the bench again.

"Well then, let us try this brew of yours, Efi. The one with the wrong herbs. Sometimes mistakes are the beginning of man's best new inventions."

"Or women's best new inventions," Gritta corrected him.

Efi handed him a clay cup of the spoiled brew. Friar Wikerus took a sip and immediately spat it on the dirt floor.

"Ugh! That is terrible!"

Appel turned and gave Efi a pointed look of disgust.

"White flowers next time, Efi, not yellow!"

Hattie, Odile, and Hilde

In which Appel stands up for the women of Les Tanneurs

I t wasn't until Sheriff Werner had led recently widowed Herr Widmer from his cell underneath the ground in the weinstube's cellars into the freezing light the early morning, that he began to appreciate the work of the three alewives of Les Tanneurs. The residents of Colmar were bundled against the sharp cold. Above them, the hard, round ball of the winter sun rose into an icy-blue sky. Below their feet, the ground sparkled with frost. Slumbering beneath the earth lay their hopes of survival for the next year: clear waters that would flow down from the great Kayserberg as soon as the thaw began and the barley kernels that would rise from the soil to become green fields of grain.

The people of Colmar looked upon Sheriff Werner with adoring eyes. The wives of several burghers approached him shyly and curtseyed with demure "thank you's" for keeping them safe from the depravities of the evil sinner. Sheriff Werner puffed out his chest as he paraded the emaciated prisoner out into the open. Herr Widmer, the henpecked husband of the late

Frau Widmer, blinked into the bright light, his first view of the sun in weeks. He was hardly more than a wraith in his baggy, tattered clothes.

"Here he is then, absolved of the sin of which he was accused." Sheriff Werner paused for effect. "Murder of his wife, and not because of adultery, either." He looked at each of the women in the crowd in turn with a severe expression. "For although she had her faults, namely gossip, and envy, she was a faithful woman to the end, eh, Widmer?" He gave the man a good-natured jab in the ribs with a well-padded elbow. Herr Widmer, after weeks of starvation underground, almost fell over. When he saw the sheriff's warning look, the prisoner pulled the corners of his mouth up into a smile.

"Oh yes, a faithful wife indeed, my Hilde."

The crowds began to thin as everyone headed to the main square, talking and laughing loudly.

"I have hot turnips to warm your hands and your bellies!" a stall vendor called out into the throng of people. Nearby, a ragged jongleur batted his tambourine in a jarringly uneven rhythm, his thin voice singing out into the crowd. A few people stopped to watch or mock, but only one or two tossed a copper coin to the man. The crowd moved forward as a single animal toward the large square, just outside Saint Martin's church, where a gallows stood. Among the crowd, Appel, Gritta, and Efi held each other's hands and walked solemnly, an island of quiet in the sea of people. Behind them trailed all twelve of Gritta's children, with Jorges crookedly taking up the rear.

The alewives had discussed the execution of Girard the night watchman and convinced each other that they must attend, though it sickened them. Gritta and Efi both felt repulsed at the thought of seeing his face again after he had nearly slit their throats, while Appel pragmatically disliked crowds and the horror of public punishment. Friar Wikerus, who was under the command of the Prior of Colmar, was not permitted to attend the execution, despite his role in apprehending the thief and murderer.

It took a good amount of time for the sheriff to quiet the crowd, and when the buzz of excitement and conversation finally dimmed, he cleared his throat and puffed out his prodigious midsection until his girdle strained against it. Next to him stood the men of the city council – burghers, guildsmen, and minor lords. Lord Frider was also standing atop the platform, looking uncomfortable. Back at his stone fortress, Lady Marguerite labored with her second child, and everyone expected the announcement of a birth (or a death) within a day or two.

"You goodmen and goodwives of Colmar have come to see that this man receives the justice that he has earned for those that he slew," Sheriff Werner yelled. "The men of the city council have all examined Girard the night watchman, son of Girard the under-butcher of Eguisheim, and found him to be a reprehensible knave who stole from God's holy church. Thus, he shall be hung from this here gallows until we deem that he has given his soul up to the mercy of God."

Appel, Gritta, and Efi waited, but Sheriff Werner turned and nodded to the young man who had drawn the short straw and received the grisly task of fitting the noose and carrying out the execution.

"What about the murders?" Efi whispered. "The sheriff did not mention that Girard killed three women."

Appel turned to Gritta and saw the look of helplessness on her friend's face. Just then, a hooded figure squeezed through the crowd and sidled up to them.

"Well," a voice whispered from beneath the deep brown cowl. "Are you going to speak up for your friends?"

The alewives turned in surprise. Friar Wikerus stood with them, disguised under his cloak. Appel set her jaw and shoved her way through the crowd toward the platform where the sheriff and the city council stood.

"Sheriff!" she yelled. "Honorable council and all of you residents of Colmar!" The hum of conversation that had arisen in the crowd stopped, and all eyes were on her. She looked back and saw the glint of light off of white teeth as Friar Wikerus grinned at her from beneath his hood.

"This man has also committed the crime of murder against three women. They may have been poor, but he ended lives that were not his to take. He will confront the souls of Hattie Jungerwald, Frau Odile, and Frau Widmer as he waits for his judgment, and they shall stand witness to his sin!"

The onlookers were agitated, and Lord Frider looked at the sheriff with a puzzled frown on his face. Clearly, the nobleman had not been informed of anything more heinous than the theft of church property.

"Er, indeed." Sheriff Werner cleared his throat and looked out over the crowd again. "To take a soul, if not in battle or not that of an infidel, is also a sin against God and one's neighbors. You were right to say so, Frau Appel."

"Witchcraft is also a sin, too!" a voice shouted from somewhere in the mob, and Appel froze, her face turning white with fear. In the audience, Gritta balled her fists and prepared to march to her friend's defense, but Friar Wikerus put a hand on her arm and whispered for her to be still.

"Now, now, those rumors were put to rest long ago," Sheriff Werner chuckled. "Let us commence with the execution of this sinner here and now."

Appel slunk back to her friends and wiped a tear from her cheek. "Someone had to stand up for them," she whispered. "Someone had to make sure this was about Hattie, Odile, and Frau Widmer – not just the gold."

"Someone has to stand up for you too, Appel. The rumors persist," Gritta muttered back.

Girard wept as the noose slipped over his head and around his neck. After a final confession, in which he begged for forgiveness from God and the church, the executioner prodded him up a ladder with an iron-tipped spear in the small of his back. After what seemed like an unnecessarily long time, the executioner kicked the ladder away, and Girard's body jerked and swung while the crowd cheered. Friar Wikerus let out a long sigh, then melted into the crowd, hurrying back to the church before he could be missed by the brethren. The three alewives quietly held each other in a long embrace. They did not watch as Girard slowly died.

The Alewives of Colmar

In which all is well that ends well

EFI CLOSED HER EYES as she walked along the patch of frosted grasses outside the walls of Colmar and drew in a deep, full drag of sweet-scented air. She remained as unsentimental as ever, but only a great fool could overlook the scent of the Rhine valley on a crisp winter day. It smelled of green things sleeping under the earth, the sharp snap of wind from the nearby river, and cold, clear ice that gilded the edges of the few remaining leaves on the elm trees. Even the brilliant white snow that clung to the sides of the hills had a scent. Borne on a crackling breeze, the fresh clean smell pushed the foul miasma of the city away as she approached the city gate where the dyer and the slaughterhouse stood side by side. As she made her way through the crowded streets toward Les Tanneurs, the smell of Colmar grew decidedly more pungent. Efi smiled. It might be smelly, but it was home.

Inside Appel's house, everyone was busy as usual. Gritta oversaw the cauldron at the great stone hearth, which bubbled away with boiling grain. Two of Gritta's lank-haired children – Efi wasn't sure of their names – played at stones in a corner near one of the street-facing windows. Appel sat on a bench, fanning herself with a cabbage leaf. Efi wryly noted the pale green edge of a second leaf sticking up from the top of the older woman's dress.

"And how did it go, Efi dear?" Appel asked. At the question, Gritta stopped stirring, dried her sweaty hands on her apron, and pulled Efi onto the bench.

"It is done," Efi said, a smile broadening her face. "I have made our first order of sale. Two barrels of small ale and one rundlet of strong brew to the cellarer of Lord Frider."

Gritta scooted closer to Efi on the bench. "And did you use the method of Friar Wikerus?"

"Indeed I did. I offered Lord Frider's cellarer slightly spoiled ale from Strassburg and then our own fresh ale, with 'the holiest water in all Alsace!'"

The three women squealed with peals of laughter and pressed Efi between them in a full-bodied embrace.

"Well done, girl! Perhaps you will prove to us that you are more than just a pretty face!"

"But if it were not for my pretty face, perhaps the cellarer would not have spoken to me at all," Efi teased. Appel stopped laughing and looked at her.

"Now, don't turn to whoring, my dear. No man will marry you if you do."

"Of course not!" Efi said hotly. "I've only given myself to one man, and I shall give myself to only one man more – my next husband. I am not such a wanton woman as to turn to other beds in my widowhood!"

Neither Efi nor Gritta noticed Appel turning bright red next to them.

Appel's house quickly transformed into a dedicated brewhouse. She moved her large table, benches, and her almost pure white washbasin upstairs, keeping the second floor as her living quarters. Her location across Trench Lane from Gritta was most convenient, but Efi had to walk from her small rented rooms in the poorest part of town to meet them, and the late hours and hard work made it apparent that something had to change. The residents of Colmar did not feel an urgent need to find a new night watchman since the previous one had proved to be a murderer and a thief, and so the streets were only patrolled by stray dogs and drunks in the evenings.

"She could live with you, could she not?" Appel asked Gritta one day as she swept the dropped grains and herbs from the floor with a twig broom.

Gritta stopped her work of measuring malted barley into a mash tun to turn and stare at her friend. "Live with me? With twelve young'uns, and eight of them still living at home? How would I ever manage? She should live with you."

"Oh." Appel dropped her broom. "No, that will never do."

"Why? You have no husband, and your sleeping floor above stairs is large enough to house a small family."

"I need my privacy."

"Privacy? What's that?"

"I need to be alone in the night."

"Whyever would you want to be alone? Do you plan to take another husband?"

"No."

"Well then, let Efi live with you. It does her no good to keep a house when she has no man or babes to live in it. And it's not safe for a young woman to live by herself. People will think she is turning to whoring. What is more, the prior and the sheriff have their eyes on you both, and who knows when they will accuse you of being witches in earnest this time."

"No, Gritta."

"But I don't understand—"

"I said no!" Appel stomped her foot, and Gritta stopped her work, startled at the sudden outburst.

"Very well, if you say so," she said. "But it would be God's work. That girl has as much sense as a courtier inside a milking shed. She needs a firm, mature hand."

"Like yours. Your hands certainly look mature to me."

Gritta looked down at her hands, then tucked them under her apron. "'Tis the work in the fields that makes them so," she muttered.

"I do not want anyone living with me. I have my own habits that I wish to keep." Appel's face was red with intensity, and

Gritta could see by the hardness in her eyes that the matter was closed for discussion.

"Very well. But she cannot live with me. I haven't the room nor the patience, and Jorges would surely become a lech."

"Well, what on earth will we do with the girl? She cannot afford to go on living alone as she does, and she hasn't enough sense to take care of herself."

"The nuns?"

"Don't be ridiculous." Appel seated herself beneath the window and took up her sewing. "It would be a waste to send such a girl to the nuns. And besides, she hasn't the money for a donation nor the temperament for piety."

"Oh, and I suppose you think you do!" Gritta snapped back.

"Who has a temperament for piety?" Efi stood on the threshold, cheeks rosy and eyes sparkling. "I only stopped by for a minute, my dears, because I have news!"

"Oh aye? And what is your news?" Gritta dipped a clay cup into a cauldron of wort and gave it a small sip.

"I am to be wed!"

Gritta dropped the cup. It fell into the wort with a sploosh and sank into the murky depths. "You're what?!" Nearby, Appel sat utterly still, face pale, sewing forgotten.

"Karl Gastwirt asked for my hand yesterday evening, and I have given consent. We shall be wed as soon as the banns are read."

Appel narrowed her eyes. "Karl Gastwirt the innkeeper? The man who is nearly twenty years your elder and has five troublemaking sons?"

"And a saucy daughter," Gritta commented. "A daughter who is older than you, Efi."

Efi tittered and waved a hand. "I don't care about that. With him, I shall have accommodation, food for my belly, and money enough to buy a new hair ribbon every other Lord's Day."

"And what dowry have you to offer?" Gritta placed her hands on her hips, which had grown more ample with the advent of the brewing.

"Not much to speak of, which is why it is a miracle that he asked me! He even said that I could continue brewing ale with you, and he would be most pleased to assist in the running of our business and provide any help that we might need so that Friar Wikerus may concentrate his attention and energies on the work of the church."

"Help, eh? Would that 'help' involve using us as his personal alewerks?"

Efi laughed again. "Indeed not – Karl doesn't wish to brew. He says that women haven't the head for business, so it would be a kindness for him to assist us and take over the management of the money. And now, I am off. Karl has given me a silver coin to have a new frock made for the wedding, and I must see Herr Tailleur about the wool cloth of it."

Efi turned and practically skipped from Appel's doorway while the two older women looked after her, their mouths hanging open in surprise.

"Well!" Gritta said. "Never mind Efi's lodgings! What are we going to do about her husband?"

"Karl Gastwirt isn't marrying that girl; he's marrying himself to our alewerks so he no longer has to pay for his ale! The fact that he is gaining a pretty and brainless wife in the bargain is just cream for his porridge!" Appel's face was red with outrage. "And besides. She can't cook worth a devil's teat!"

Gritta looked with surprise at her pious friend's second sudden outburst of the day. "What are we going to do about it, then?"

Appel pushed the sleeves of her woolen dress to her elbows and took up her mash paddle, giving it a few expert thrusts like a pikeman.

"We're the alewives of Colmar, and let no man think he can take what's ours. And Efi is ours!"

"So, does this mean she can live with you?"

Appel turned to Gritta. "Old friend, never have I been more sure of something in my life. Yes, Efi can live with me if it means she will spurn that bloated, flatulent crook of an innkeeper! How dare he try to take that innocent girl for himself. And our livelihood!"

"Very good." Gritta nodded. "Let us go and find Friar Wikerus then, to have him council Efi away from this unwise decision."

"Indeed!" Appel declared, and she marched from her house into the rapidly waning light of the winter afternoon, still brandishing her mash paddle. Gritta followed slowly, closing the door behind her. As she began to walk away, she heard a whisper from a nearby pine tree.

"Pssst! Gritta! Did it work?"

Gritta looked left and right before turning to the tree to answer.

"Yes, dear, it worked. Now run along to your house and remember to look sad when Appel forbids you to marry Karl Gastwirt."

"I will indeed, Frau Gritta, though it may be hard, for surely I would never accept such a man."

"Surely not." Gritta nodded, although she truly doubted her own assurance. Young, old, short, or tall, Efi looked at men the way Jorges looked at a full pitcher of wine.

"Gritta!" She heard Appel shout from down the lane. "Are you coming?"

"I'm coming!" Gritta called back, and she smiled as Efi disappeared around the house and out of sight. She took a moment to gaze down Trench Lane. The mud between the ruts in the hard-packed dirt had frozen into lumpy brown ice, and the remaining leaves that clung to the bare branches of the plum trees scraped against each other with a thin, papery sound. As the twilight ripened in the square, the residents of Les Tanneurs pulled their cloaks tight around their shoulders and hurried into their homes.

For so many years during the Great Pestilence, Gritta, like everyone in her city, dreaded the onset of winter: the bitter cold, coupled with the suffering of her friends and loved ones, was a terrifying prospect. But this year, she felt different. Warm candlelight twinkled from the cracks between the shuttered windows of the houses, and from the nearby square, she could hear a woman singing as she went about her evening chores. Gritta knew that this year, unlike the previous years, her winter would be filled with the chatter and gossip of her friends, the balm of her children's love, and the warm, nutty scent of the ale as it fermented in the barrels.

A rare, unpracticed smile spread across her face. She was a part of a sisterhood now. She had a way to earn a wage and feed her family, and the Great Pestilence, with its horrors and heartbreak, was behind her.

The future looked bright.

THE END

Join me!

In which the reader is invited into the community

D ID YOU ENJOY *The Alewives*? Other readers would love to know if the exploits of Gritta, Appel, and Efi are a worthwhile read, and your positive review is one of the most effective ways to support independent authors like me. Please leave a review or recommend *The Alewives* to your book club.

Want to receive semi-regular updates on my own journey learning to brew gruit ale, read reviews of my favorite small-breweries, and learn the history of ale, not just in Europe but in the near and far east where it originated? Join my mailing list! Here's what I can promise: you will get a laugh, you will learn something, and you might find a good deal on another medieval mystery book from a fellow indie author. You will also receive *Nasira*, the free prequel novella to *The Two Daggers* series for free. Sign up at https://www.elizabethrandersen.com

- Find photos of hikes and daily author life at my Instagram: @elizabethrandersen and Facebook: https://www.facebook.com/ERAndersenBooks

- Follow me on Twitter for nerdy medieval history facts: @E_R_A_writes

- Watch me try to explain the weird, wonderful world of Medieval life on my TikTok channel: @elizabethrandersen

Author's note

In which the author explains herself

I T WAS OVER A very fine ale that I came up with the idea for *The Alewives*. Like my previous books, current events influenced my creativity and decision-making. We were two years into the COVID-19 pandemic, disease-weary like the rest of the world, and perched on the edge of the Russo-Ukrainian war. My son was required to complete grades 3 and 4 from home via remote learning and the home renovation that had been planned for years (saving, designing, and arguing with local bureaucrats, etc.) began, so there were times when our house had no insulation and only partial electricity for nine months, and even an entire summer with no roof over our heads. I was just finishing the third book in my medieval Palestinian epic, *The Two Daggers*, but the story, a crusade-era drama was getting darker and darker, as was my general outlook on life. I needed something to pull me back into the light. I needed some humor.

I needed the alewives.

In the summer of 2022, I embarked on a research trip to Marseilles in order to understand the locations for my 4th and 5th books in *The Two Daggers* series. The plan was to continue to Avignon, but at the time, wildfires and overcrowded festivals made it impossible to get near the city. I changed course, taking my dear friend Katie with me to Alsace at the eastern edge of France. This wasn't my first time in Alsace, but it was the time I really saw it – not for being French or German, or a disputed territory, or even for its tragic suffering during the world wars, but for being *Alsatian*.

Alsace is the territory along the Rhine River that has been contested since the 17th century, trapped in a game of tug-of-war between Germany and France for hundreds of years. Why? Alsace has fertile soil for growing grain and for cultivating some of the best wine grapes in the region. It's also situated along a major waterway for carrying goods and soldiers. Its status of being located along a feisty border makes Alsace "castle country," and it hosts some of the oldest, most incredible medieval castles still standing, and all because the rulers of the region were trying to either keep the Germans out or the French out.

But before the 17th century, Alsace was independent, with its own rulers and customs. The ten largest cities of Alsace formed what became known as the "Decapole" – free imperial cities that swore allegiance to the Holy Roman Emperor himself with no middlemen to take their own share in rents and labor from the local population. This coveted status was rare at the time. The status of Free Imperial City could be bargained for, won, or granted, and it could also be taken away. The cities and towns of Alsace developed a rich culture based on the bounty that they were able to pull from the ground, and they are still known for producing the finest wines in Germany and France. But they also brewed ale, and this is what really interested me.

Before beer became what it is now – a shelf-stable beverage that is high in alcohol content and whose consumption is limited to people over a certain age – people drank "small ale." This kind of brew was less alcoholic (only about 2-4%) and was used to for every day consumption that would allow people to stay hydrated without being constantly intoxicated. These ales were brewed without the addition of hops as the primary bittering agent, which would become popular many years later, and so they spoiled quickly. Women were responsible for brewing in their homes in order to sustain their families with hydration that was fermented enough to kill dangerous bacteria, and, of course, they might make something a little stronger for special occasions. If the family didn't drink everything, these women were allowed to sell the excess ale from their homes or in the markets if they wished to earn some money for their families. At least, that is how things went until the mid-14th century. For more on what happened to the ale and beer trade, well...there's a mystery to be solved in the next book, and the Alewives of Colmar will be on the case!

S'Gilt!

E.R.A.

Acknowledgements

In which proper accreditation is made

THIS WAS A HARD book to write. This was harder than the first three books in my series about the Siege of Acre, which was violent, sad, required more research, more editing, and more words. But this book...this one needed to shine a little light when I thought there was nothing left in the world but darkness. So, to the people who helped, there's no way I can truly tell you how much you have meant to me in 2022.

First of all, I need to thank Jordan and Soren. Even thought things haven't been easy (and I keep a strange schedule and talk to myself a lot) you've always believed in *The Alewives*. A very close second goes to the two amazing editors at The History Quill who ensured accuracy and readability: Craig Hillsley and Sarah Dronfield. Although I've never met him personally, I owe a debt to the meticulous and passionate research of Patrick McGovern, whose council with Sam Calagione of Dogfish Head brewery produced Midas Touch, which is my all-time favorite brew. It truly tastes like liquid gold. If you haven't done it yet, find yourself a Midas and drink it while reading *Ancient Brews* (McGovern, W.W. Norton & Co., 2017).

So many thanks to my dad, Louis Roscoe III and my little brother, Christian Roscoe, for their advice - both solicited and otherwise. As homebrewers, they helped unlock the mystery of fermentation to me, and even let me try weird and often terrible-tasting experiments with their equipment. I also want to thank my pepé, Albert Clifford "Cliff" Cloutier, whose unorthodox brewing methods were the stuff of dubious legend and even more uncertain taste, but his passion was contagious and his legacy is still strong.

I also owe a debt of gratitude to François, who cautioned me to treat the Alsatian people and culture with the dignity and depth of research that they deserve. Right now, I hope he is floating on a boat somewhere in the Calanques, without a care in the world. Many thanks also to Carol F., ARC reader extraordinaire, who saved me from a mistake at the last minute. More thanks to the friends who supported me during a truly difficult time which happened to coincide with the creation of this book: Jim K., Jordan C., Mariko L., Michael S., Lauren C., Jon S., and to the wonderful members of my Medieval Author's group, Eilish Quinn, Brenda Vinal-Mogal, and especially to the incomparable M.J. Porter, who is sweet and kind and writes the bloodiest, goriest fiction about Saxon England you'll ever read, and to the one and only Kelly Evans, who is the definition of a sassy woman, and writes about them with moxie and expertise. You two have held me up this year.

Finally, to Katie Hendrickson (Katers), my oldest friend. We've known each other since babyhood, have been through ups, downs, births, deaths, weddings, breakups, fights, and laughter. Thank you for always being there, even when the darkness overtakes me sometimes.

And to my readers: I hope you were entertained, educated, perplexed, and laughed a little. You make my world go 'round.

E.R.A.

About Elizabeth R. Andersen

In which the author introduces herself

Elizabeth R. Andersen is an independent historical fiction author living in the beautiful Pacific Northwest of the United States. Her debut novel, *The Scribe*, launched in July of 2021.

Elizabeth is passionate about reviving (and eating) historical recipes, reading and supporting other indie authors, and exploring the stunning Cascade mountains.

- Join Elizabeth's monthly newsletter and receive *Nasira*, the free prequel novella to *The Two Daggers* series for free. Sign up at https://www.elizabethrandersen.com

- Find photos of hikes and daily author life at Elizabeth's Instagram: @elizabethrandersen and Facebook: https://www.facebook.com/ERAndersenBooks

- Follow Elizabeth on Twitter for nerdy medieval history facts: @E_R_A_writes

- Watch Elizabeth try to explain the weird, wonderful world of Medieval life on her TikTok channel: @elizabethrandersen

Also by Elizabeth R. Andersen

In which we discover that the author also writes other books

The Scribe

A spoiled nobleman, a Mamluk soldier, and a brilliant orphan. When war threatens their city, will they overcome prejudice to work together?

As the sun begins to set on the crusades in 13th century Palestine, Henri of Maron will encounter the greatest challenge of his life. Angry and indulged, young Henri's father forced him to live and train among men who hated him for what he was - half-French, half-Arab, and wealthier than any other private citizen in the city. Robbed of his childhood and steeped in cruelty, an unexpected encounter with a kindly scribe will present Henri with an opportunity he is not sure he wanted: a chance to rediscover his humanity and possibly save a life along the way. When forced to choose sides between the knights that he idolizes and what he knows to be right, Henri must overcome his greatest enemy: himself.

Book one in *The Two Daggers* series, *The Scribe* pulls readers along as history sweeps three young people toward the infamous Siege of Acre, and toward each other.

* * * * * *"Andersen slowly and expertly weaves their stories together into a thrilling tale of deceit and intrigue that kept me guessing until the last chapters."*

* * * * * *"Attention to historical detail is amazing, and your really feel yourself transported back 600 years to a climate filled with tension. Highly recommend."*

* * * * * "The story is compelling and characters well developed. The historical perspective is new and thought provoking. I am looking forward to the sequel!"

The Land of God

Pain. His sister's screams. And a beautiful face in the jeering crowd. When Henri of Maron woke, he had only a few memories of his brutal flogging, but he knew the world had changed. *He* had changed.

Now, as he grapples with the fallout from his disastrous decisions, war with the Mamluk army looms closer. To convince the city leaders to take the threat seriously, Henri and the grand master of the Templars must rely on unlikely allies and bold risks to avoid a siege.

Meanwhile, Sidika is trying to find a way to put her life back together. When she is forced to flee her home, her chance encounters with a handsome amir and a strangely familiar old woman will have consequences for her future.

The Land of God weaves the real historical figures with rich, complex characters and an edge-of-seat plot. Readers who enjoyed the *Brethren* series by Robyn Young and *The Physician* by Noah Gordon will appreciate this immersive tale set in the Middle East in the Middle Ages.

The Amir

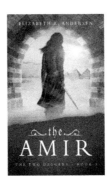

Acre has fallen.

In the frantic days after the Mamluk army brutally sacked their city, Sidika and Emre find themselves in Egypt at the house of an ambitious amir to Sultan al-Ashraf Khalil. Emre, reinstated to his position in the Mamluk army, plays a dangerous game, pitting the sultan's amirs against each other in a bid to increase his influence in the royal court. Sidika, captured as a slave, can only think of Henri and escape. But when Emre comes up with a risky plan to help her flee Cairo, how far is she willing to go for her freedom?

Henri, now living in Francia among hostile relatives, dreams of finding Sidika and ransoming her, but he cannot avoid a nobleman's duties: arranged marriage awaits him. As he attempts to settle into his new life, a group of outcasts arrives in Maron, causing an uproar. By protecting them, Henri does what he knows is right, but the consequences could be deadly.

Love, lust, revenge, and loss push Henri, Sidika, and Emre
toward adulthood in the third book in *The Two Daggers* series,
following them through social and political turbulence at the
sunset of the Levantine crusades.

The Marquis of Maron *(coming summer 2023)*

All seems lost for Henri of Maron as he hides, gravely injured, with a mysterious hermit in the forests of his ancestral homeland. The betrayal of his family is heart-rending, the revenge by his uncle Gaspard, complete. When a villager describes a waterfall guarded by a holy man who can cure the sick, Henri decides to set out to seek a miracle. But outside the forest, more danger awaits as his murderous relatives gain the help of King Philippe to put a price on Henri's head.

Half a world away, Sidika's plans for escape from Egypt have failed and she remains a slave in a noble house. Her freedom is eventually assisted by an unlikely ally, and she knows what she must do: she must find Henri. She sets out on a voyage across oceans and continents to find the man who she knows to be her future.

Emre is also fighting his way from Egypt in pursuit of Sidika and redemption for the pain and suffering he caused. As he follows her trail, he will learn the dangerous secret of the two daggers, why they are sought by so many, and why the holder of the daggers has the power to change the past.

Filled with adventure, romance, and treachery, *The Marquis of Maron* brings readers to the doorstep of the final chapter in this 5-book series as Henri, Sidika, and Emre struggle for survival in 13th century France.

Printed in Great Britain
by Amazon